THE REGIME

FRANK HUGHES

Library of Congress Control Number: 2023943542
            Paperback: 978-1-961119-38-3
            eBook: 978-1-961119-39-0

CONTENTS

"THE PRESENT"

"Huh huh huh no, no!" The Sound coming from a white male dressed in a bath robe and silk pajama pants. He has blood leaking from a gash on his arm. He scarcely runs through a wooded area not too far off in a distance from a plush mansion in the background. The sound of gunfire is heard coming from inside the mansion. "There he is!" is what one of two men inside the house brandishing firearms in hand yells out. "Where? I can't see him!" The second man with firearm in hand cries out. They're both Caucasian, dressed in black suits complete with matching red ties. They make their way down one of the many halls of the manor. They have their guns drawn and are anxious to fire. With sweat dripping from their heads profusely, they breathe heavily as they creep down the hall. As they step forward, the crackling in the wood grain floor frightens them somewhat, but they are determined to find who they are after. A crackling noise peaks through in the background. They turn around to see what it is. Suddenly from behind the two men, a black male of Haitian descent appears dressed in a fatigue green trench coat, armed with knives in both hands. He takes one of the blades and throws it swiftly into the lower back of the guard on his right side. As the guard falls to his knees, the Haitian man now armed with one blade now charges toward the guard on his left side. As the guard with his pistol drawn turns around, he's too late. The assailant lodges his second knife into the guard's chest. As the assailant pulls the blade from the guard's impaled torso, his facial expression changes from fear to acceptance. He falls to his knees and eventually flat on his face and stomach. The guard who took a knife to his lower back tries to reach for the firearm that he dropped when he was attacked, but the assailant walks over and kicks the gun away. The guard looks up and asks "Who are you?", but the mysterious man does not answer, he just walks away. The guard lays on the floor in fear and unable to move as he waits for the assailant to finish him off. He looks around and notices that no one is around, and breathes out a sigh of relief.

The assailant walks out onto the outdoor patio on the second floor. He looks out into the wooded area where the white male dressed in his bath robe ran to. He spots the man down a trail he has made from the blood leaking from his wounded arm. The assailant hops over the balcony and drops a good fifteen feet. He looks ahead and spots his target further down the woods. The assailant then sprints off at an impressive rate. He follows the blood trail left by his victim, who is in shock as he frantically runs through the wooded area. The assailant is sprinting at full speed after him. The man in his plush robe is breathing heavily in fear as he continues to run and stumble. He looks behind him again and notices the assailant is no longer behind him. He comes to a stop at a tree and tries to take a rest. As he hunches over to catch his breath, he coughs up phlegm as sweat begins to drip from his face. He continues to look around for the assailant, but there's no one in sight for him to see. He smiles as he turns around. "Ha, Ha, Ha I knew those old fools wouldn't send anyone worthy of taking me out. Ha, I'll get those bastards." The man says. Suddenly the sound of leaves crunching coming from behind him disturbs his relief. He turns abruptly all while quieting his panting breaths. He takes his right hand and rubs it over his face. He continues to look around, but still does not see anyone around, just the wilderness of the forest. He breathes out and sighs. Suddenly from behind him the assailant appears. The man notices the assailant's shadowy figure on a tree in front of him. His eyes and mouth begin to widen. Suddenly he begins to tremble in fear. The assailant grabs the man by his shoulder and quickly pulls him in close as he swiftly swipes his blade across the victim's neck. Blood squirts out as the man grabs his throat and falls to his knees. He desperately tries to gasp for air, but it's too late. The man eventually stops struggling to breathe as his eyes begin to roll back and he accepts his fate. He eventually falls flat on his face and stomach. The assailant stares down at his recent victim. Suddenly a raspy voice of German accent comes through on his earpiece. "Lamar, come in." The voice says. He reaches up and presses a button on top. "Here" he answers. "Is it done?" The voice on the other line asks. "Yes" Lamar answers. "Okay. You know what you have to do, see you when you get back. Over and out." The voice says. "Over and out" Lamar

says in response. He then turns around and walks away from the body as
the scene fades.

"THE RIDE BACK"

The interior of a dimly lit three row wide aircraft in flight opens the scene. Lamar sits in his window seat and stares out his window and watches the clear blue sky with a few clouds as the plane passes through them. Then within an instant, a flash of his recent victim comes to mind. The image of the victim gasping for his last breath irritates him somewhat. He closes his eyes and shakes his head while rubbing his hand over his face slowly. As he opens his eyes and breathes out a sigh of relief. He then closes his eyes again and takes a deep breath. Suddenly he hears "Sir would like a snack and beverage?" The flight attendant asks. He remains silent for a moment and then answers, "I'll take some water." The stewardess then hands him a bottle of water. "Enjoy sir." She tells him. "Thank you." He says in response. Lamar opens the bottle of water and takes a big gulp. He then screws the cap back on, sits the bottle down, lounges back in his seat and closes his eyes.

"SAFE HAVEN"

The mountains of the Northwestern Territory countryside of Canada seem so peaceful and quiet, but deep down within this place, it has seen its shares of violence and havoc. This is where the organization better known as The Regime resides. This is where the high class group of assassins is breaded. Taken from broken homes, group homes and orphanages around the world. The kids, who are eventually grown into elite assassins, come here to train, develop and live. It is here where they leave all the pain, torment and neglect from their parents or prior circumstances behind and become tools of a secret society hidden from plain sight.

An all black luxury car pulls up to what looks like a rundown manor. Lamar steps out the car with his bag in hand dressed down in a black trench coat and suite. He walks up to the door of the facility. He stands and waits for the driver to pull off. Once the car leaves, he reaches into his coat pocket and pulls out a key. He inserts the key into the keyhole of the door, turns the knob, and makes his way inside. The place seems quiet at first, but as Lamar goes through a second set of doors and makes his way inside the manor, the room is filled with action of young prodigies in training. Some

The Regime

are taking target practice, hand to hand combat, wiring explosives and last but not least The Regime's ultimate weapon of choice, knives and blades. The Regime lives by two traits; show no mercy and no emotion, for these two characteristics will hinder one's judgment.

"Lamar you're back!" A black male, who is of African American descent, says. "Valentine" Lamar says in return. The two of them greet one another and shake hands. "So how was the assignment?" Valentine asks. "Well I made it back didn't I?" Lamar answers with a blank stare on his face. "Yes you did convincingly. Kid, I'm impressed. You're getting almost as good as me!" Valentine responds with a sinister grin on his face. "Well he still has a long way to go, before he reaches your level Valentine!" says a white male of German descent standing at the top of the stairs. "Kristian! Good to see you!" Valentine says. "Like wise old friend." Kristian replies. Valentine smirks and turns back to Lamar. "I'll see you around kid." He says as he walks off. "Lamar, come, we have things to discuss." Kristian says. Lamar makes his way upstairs. He and Kristian walk with one another. Kristian pulls out a cigar from the pocket on the left side of his shirt. He puts it up to his mouth, lights it and begins to puff on it. "You know kid you're a natural. The fastest rising prodigy I've trained. You seem to have also created a new fan in Valentine. Ha Ha don't worry kid, he thrives off competition. Sometimes I swear he loves trying to be the best more than he loves his own wife." Kristian says as he takes a puff from his cigar. "What a treat!" he says after blowing smoke out. "Kristian always seems to be nonchalant."

Lamar thinks to himself. Lamar doesn't say much around Kristian. He just listens and absorbs the words and knowledge Kristian speaks. After all, he is The Regime's most highly decorated assassin throughout their history of existence.

Lamar gets to his room, from behind Kristian follows. "Okay kid, your next mission will take place very soon. You will have at least two days to prepare for it. Get some rest; briefing will start immediately in the Morning." Kristian explains as he exits the room and closes the door behind.

Once Kristian leaves and the room gets quiet, Lamar reflects back on his most recent kill once again. The way his victim was running in fear. He recalls the man trembling in fear right before he met his fate. He cannot bare the thought of the situation taking place again throughout his mind as he shakes his head. After many kills he has made for The Regime, Lamar has never really liked killing those who saw their death coming to them. He prefers it to be quick, painless and unnoticeable, but they're always painful whether it's for them or him living with the guilt. The Regime could care less just as long as the job is done without leaving a trace for unwanted attention.

"IN MY SLEEP"

It's just after nightfall as Lamar stares out the window of his room and looks over the peaceful landscapes of the Canadian Rocky Mountains. Here is where he reminisces his times as a kid in the slums of the violent and crime filled city of Detroit. He reflects about all those years spent in the group home. His mood begins to change. He goes into an emotional phase of sadness. As he stares out the window a tear begins to form in his right eye, and begins to slowly roll down the side of his cheek. This is something that the regime does not allow, because they feel it's a distraction to the assassin's judgment for when it's time to execute their targets, but this is an emotion Lamar has learned to hide from the rest of the outside world. He only shares his sadness with himself, making him all the more dangerous.

Lamar wipes away his tears, walks over to his bed and lies down. From here it slowly becomes darker. Once he closes his eyes, he begins to hear the voices of his victims come into play. A collage of screams, cries and painful agony disturbs him for a minute. Then within an instant they stop.

Two Years ago. A young Lamar is seen walking through the lobby of an expensive restaurant. He walks over to the bar, and takes a seat. The bartender comes over. "What will it be?" The bartender asks. "Club soda with lemon" Lamar tells him. The bartender walks away and prepares Lamar's drink. Lamar reaches into his pocket and pulls out a small photograph. It's a picture of a white male, possibly of Italian descent. In either his late thirties or early forties. Lamar quickly puts the photo back into his pocket as the bartender walks back over to him with his drink. "Anything else sir?" the bartender asks. "No this is all." Lamar replies. The bartender then walks away and serves the next customer. Lamar looks up and notices the bartender's next customer is his target from the photograph. Lamar's facial expression remains calm as he stares down his prey. Once his target looks back up; Lamar picks up his drink and casually sips from the glass while staring down at a newspaper. "Is that today's paper?" Lamar looks up and notices the question came from his target. "No its yesterday's actually". Lamar responds. "Hmm well that's something different." The man says. "I like to live at my own pace." Lamar says. "That's understandable." The man replies as he takes his glass and drinks his beverage. The man places his glass down, pulls out his wallet and places a one hundred dollar bill on the counter. "Keep the change." He says as he puts away his wallet and walks off. Lamar's eyes follow the man as he makes his way to the restroom. Lamar knows it's time to make his move. He soon pulls out a twenty-dollar bill and places it on the counter. "Thanks for the drink." He says to the bartender as he walks off. "Anytime." The bartender says. Lamar casually makes his way to the restroom area. He looks around to make sure no one else is around. He walks inside. He makes his way over to the sink area and turns on the faucet. As the water runs, Lamar notices that the stalls are empty. His eyes cut to the left. Then suddenly from his right side his target appears brandishing a twenty five-caliber pistol. He puts it up to Lamar's temple. "Who are you?" he asks. Lamar stares in the mirror back at the man, but he doesn't answer. "Well it doesn't matter who you are, I know who sent you." The man says. Lamar still does not respond. "So they send you? What's in the newspaper?" The man asks as he notices the paper on the sink. "Open it!" he says. Lamar doesn't do anything; he just stares at the man's reflection off the mirror. "Open it!" the man yells out as he pulls back the hammer on the pistol. Lamar opens it revealing a twenty two-caliber pistol. The man looks down at it and says "Toss it to the floor" Lamar takes the small pistol and tosses it behind him. The man keeps his pistol aimed at the back of Lamar's head as he leans down to pick the pistol up. "So this is what you were going use?" he asks. "No. I was thinking something a little more quiet and painful." Lamar says as a small sharp edged knife ejects out from his right handed sleeve and he quickly turns around and grabs the mans hand with the pistol still in his grip and swiftly slices across the man's wrist causing him to drop the gun. Lamar then spins and maneuvers behind the man while pulling him in close. He quickly swipes the blade across the man's neck and drives the blade up through his neck region under the chin. Lamar holds the blade inside the wound as the man panics and tries to fight off the attack, but it's too late. The man gives up and faints. Lamar shakes his head in shame. He then drags his victim's body into one of the bathroom stalls and sits him on the stool. He exits from the stall and closes the door.

He then walks over to the sink area and picks up the twenty two caliber pistol as well as the victim's twenty five caliber chrome pistol. He cleans the guns off and wraps them in the newspaper; walks over to the trash can and dumps the paper in. He washes his hands thoroughly, dries them and exits the restroom. As he steps out he looks around, turns to his right and exits the building through the back door.

"ABRUPT WAKING"

Lamar wakes from his sleep abruptly. As he sits up he rubs his hands over his face. As he closes his eyes, the image of the victim in his dream appears. He shakes his head. He then steps out his bed and walks over to the window and stares out at the view of the beautiful mountains in front of him. This is his usual routine throughout most nights. The nightmares of his past kills constantly haunt him. As he stares out the window, a sense of peace comes to mind as he takes a deep breath. He bows his head and smirks a little before walking back over to his bed and lying down.

"WHEN THE MORNING COMES"

After a few hours have passed, the universal alarm in the compound goes off. As the sound of the vibrant bell rings throughout the manor, Lamar is already awake taking his morning stare out the window. As he stares his room door opens, and Kristian steps in. "Always alert kid, that's good; whether you know it or not, that's one trait that can save your life. You know I came to this place nearly thirty years ago. I've seen many things over time. Even things I don't agree with, but one thing this place teaches is how to get past those feelings of disagreement," Kristian explains as he pauses and breathes out. Lamar then turns and asks "disagreements like what?" "As time goes on you'll see" Kristian says as he walks over to Lamar and hands him a manila folder. "Here's your next target. Take this phone, I will call you and give you direct instructions on what to do." He says. Lamar takes the folder opens it and looks at the picture of his next target inside. He's an elderly man with fierce cut eyes. Lamar can tell just by the picture that the individual has a great amount of power, but with secrecy. Lamar wants to ask who the man is, but he remembers what the Regime has taught him. "Do and don't ask." Kristian walks to the door and looks back "You'll need to be ready in the next twenty minutes." He says as he proceeds to exit.

"THE CAR RIDE"

Lamar gets into the luxury car that is waiting outside to pick him up. The ride through the range is always peaceful and thought seeking. Lamar enjoys the jagged ranges of mountains lit up by the sun sitting in the clear sky. As the car passes through the scenery, Lamar sits and thinks about his mission. He usually does this before all of missions. He is now mentally prepared for the task at hand.

"HIGH NOON"

Shanghai China, a city of many people and mass scenery. Lamar marvels at the sight of the buildings within view from his hotel room, but he doesn't let the beauty of the city blind him for too long. He remembers what's at hand. He's waiting to receive a call from Kristian. He thinks to himself "Something's wrong, he's more than thirty minutes late." As this thought comes to mind, the phone finally rings. Lamar picks up and listens. "Sorry I took so long, had to take extra precautions. Okay here's the plan. You will enter the building directly across the street from the hotel. The target is located directly southeast of where you're at now. Then you will go into the custodial closet on the eighth floor. There will be a marked custodial bin and uniform inside, inside of the bin will be everything you need. There will be a phone inside, press the six key and it will automatically dial out a number for you to reach me. I will give you further instructions from there." Kristian says. The phone then hangs up.

Lamar has followed through on the instructions that Kristian has given him. He pulls the phone from the custodial bin. He flips the phone open and dials the six key. The phone dials out the number to reach Kristian.

When he answers Lamar does not say a word, he just listens. "Okay the next step is simple. Take the elevator to the forty-fifth floor. From here you can take the freight elevator to the roof, but I recommend taking the stairs, because there aren't any cameras in that region. From there you'll find your target in the east corner of the building across on the sixty- seventh floor. Approximately at noon you will get a signal. From there I want you to do nothing except execute." Kristian says. The phone then abruptly hangs up.

Lamar finally makes it to the roof. He gazes over the edge of the building and looks over. He then takes a look at his watch. It's around eight forty five in the morning. He knows he's early, which is always good for his advantage in the particular situation. This way he knows he can take his time, which he does. He pulls out a binocular scope and scans the neighboring building. He then finds his target's room in the exact location Kristian has told him. Lamar then breaks out a case. He opens it. He pulls out parts of a sniper rifle and quickly assembles them together. He then sets up a great position to execute from without being seen from others in the adjacent buildings. He then pulls out the manila envelope that Kristian had given him. He opens it pulls out the picture of his target and examines the photograph again. On it is an elderly Chinese man, who may be fairly chunky given by the characteristics of his face. As Lamar continues to stare at the photo, thoughts began racing through his mind. He thinks to himself. "Who is this person, what does he do? Why is he being targeted?" He says to himself. He knows such thoughts as these can get him killed if revealed to the Regime. He quickly dismisses them and focuses back on the task. He takes a look at his watch again and sees that close to two hours have passed. He looks through the scope of the high quality rifle. Despite the cold winds blowing against his skin, he is prepared mentally to wait for the signal Kristian will send him.

"EXECUTION TIME"

It's just around ten forty-five AM, when Lamar notices movement inside the room of his target. He sees the light glowing throughout the room, but the target is not alone. He has company, a young female who doesn't seem to be of age. Lamar looks through the scope to try to get a great execution shot. As he looks through the scope he looks around the room for small details, like something that looks unusual. As time goes by Lamar knows what's going on in the room is something that is not age appropriate for the young lady in the room with the elderly man. As Lamar continues to search, he notices in the corner widow of the building, a table with a few books and a phone. He sees that it's the only clear opening for a shot along with the perfect timing.

It's around eleven- fifty-five AM when the target's company finally leaves, but before she departs, she does something mysterious. She walks over toward the table and leaves a key card on the table where the phone is. Lamar notices it immediately. "That's it, that's the signal!" He says to himself. After the target's company exits, Lamar notices the light on the phone flickering. It's ringing. The target then walks over to the phone to answer it. He picks it up, but hears nothing but silence. Lamar sees this and proceeds to pull the trigger. "Pop" the bullet projectile travels at a high speed. It goes through the glass with ease right into the side of the target's head. The impact from the shot flips the target's body over with tremendous force from the bullet lodged into his brain. Lamar quickly breaks down the rifle and puts it back in the case and moves quickly from the roof to the stairs that lead down to the freight elevator. He puts the rifle case back in the custodial bin and locks it in the storage closet. While leaving, a security officer notices him and attempts to stop him. "Hey stop right there!" the security officer yells out in Chinese dialogue. Lamar does as he says. "What are you doing here? Custodians are not allowed in this area during these hours." He says. Lamar remains silent. The officer then pulls out his baton. He walks up close to Lamar and points it in the bottom of Lamar's back. "I asked you question!" The officer yells out. Lamar quickly spins around quickly grabbing the end of the baton with ease and snatches it away. The officer attempts to throw a punch, but Lamar dodges it and grabs the officer's arm and slings him face first into the wall. Lamar then asks the officer in Chinese dialogue. "How many officers are on the ground floor?" The officer then answers "Six on the floor, two outside in the front." Lamar then says "Thank you. Sorry but I have to." "What?" The officer asks. "This" Lamar says as he delivers a swift chop to the back of the officer's neck. The officer falls unconsciously. Lamar proceeds to exit down to the ground floor.

"GROUND LEVEL"

"Bing" the sound of the elevator coming to a stop opens the scene. Lamar steps through the elevator doors as soon as they open. He looks to his left and to his right. He is very aware of the situation that may occur if he is discovered. He rips off the custodian jumpsuit and tosses it in the trash can right before he gets to the lobby. Now dressed in an all black suit and navy blue tie, he begins to walk to the front door to exit, but to no surprise the security officers appear and confront him. "Stop right there!" They yell out. The officers in this particular building are armed with automatic handguns. They have them drawn and aimed sternly. Lamar didn't have any knowledge about the officer up stairs having his radio on, during their confrontation, but it doesn't matter the officers have no idea of what they are in for. Lamar puts his hands up. The first officer, who is a heavy set fellow walks over to Lamar and attempts to grab his hands so he can restrain him. Lamar sees an opening and goes for it. As soon as the officer's hand makes contact with Lamar's wrist, Lamar turns around quickly and grabs the officer's gun and takes it from him. He quickly hits the officer in his stomach and turns his body so that he facing the other officers, but there is one problem. The officers are blocking the door, but to no avail. Lamar throws the guard face first into the crowd of his fellow officers. As the guard is falling forward Lamar runs up his back and dives through the glass doors. The guards begin to fire, but they're too late. Lamar gets away quickly. One of the guards grabs his radio and calls for the local police to come as Lamar escapes, but by the time they arrive Lamar is long gone.

"OUTSIDE ENVIRONMENT"

Lamar quickly makes it up the street away from the may-lay. As he makes his way through the crowds, the local police arrive. He tries to be discreet, but a Haitian in a Chinese environment, he just doesn't quite fit in. The police spot him without a problem. They surround him with their foreign cars. They step out and immediately draw their weapons. "Put your hands up" they yell out. Lamar does exactly what they tell him. One officer approaches, as he gets closer. Lamar notices he is tensely holding his weapon. The officer reaches out to restrain Lamar, but just like the security officers back at the office building, the officer has no chance from the start. Lamar grabs the officer and flips him over onto his back, the other officers surrounding draw their weapons and began firing. Multiple shots ring out, but Lamar possesses the special ability due to his training with the Regime, of being able to read the officers muscles and reacting seconds before they fire. As the officers fire off shots, Lamar quickly dodges the bullets. While he does this, he pulls out a few of his special little friends, (Small sharp throwing knives). He throws out the first to the officer on his left, striking him in the side of his neck. The officer falls within an instant. Lamar looks to his right and notices the officer on that side widens his eyes with fear, but he keeps firing his gun hoping to hit Lamar with one of the bullets he has left, but he falls to his knees suddenly while looking down and noticing he has been hit in the chest as blood leaks from the wound. The officer tries to contain the bleeding, but he soon meets his fate. He goes into shock and passes out. The remaining officers in front of Lamar soon run out of ammo. They pull out their batons and rush toward Lamar. The first two officers approach Lamar at high speed, but this is a big mistake. They swing at him with their sticks. Lamar catches the stick from the first officer to reach him, once Lamar grabs the baton; he does an acrobatic spin to relinquish it from the officer. Once this happens, Lamar takes the baton and swings it at the officer's knee and breaking it. The officer falls to one knee. Lamar notices the second officer coming; he looks down at the first officer who is on one knee and looks back up toward the other officer. He kicks the officer who's down on one knee in the chest as soon as the second officer gets close. The first officer falls back and bumps into the second officer. The second officer reacts by trying to catch his comrad. Once this happens Lamar quickly spins around and gets behind the second officer. Once he is in position; he quickly swings the baton and hits the officer on the clavicle. The impact of the strike disables him quickly and he falls to the ground holding his shoulder. "Ahh" he yells out. Without waiting for more officers to arrive. Lamar turns around and takes off. His speed is no match for them to catch up to him. He's able to make his way through the crowded streets without an officer in sight, as he heads back to the hotel.

Lamar gets back to his hotel room. He opens the door and looks around to make sure everything is just the way he left it. He then goes into the bathroom and turns on the faucet. He dips his hands into the water and washes them. He cups his hands and splashes the water on his face. He then looks up and stares at himself in the mirror. Flashes of his last actions begin to come to mind. The shot from his rifle that took out his target, the knocking out the security officer, the bones cracking and breaking on the police officers. "Why am I doing all of this?" He asks himself quietly. Suddenly His phone rings. He already knows who it is. He picks the phone up and presses the answer key as he puts it up to his ear. "Looks like everything is taken care of; there's still one thing I need you to do." Kristian begins giving Lamar a list of things to do. "I want you to get a change of clothes. Next put all of the clothes you have on now in a bag along with the phone that we are speaking on currently. Then take the bag and dispose of it the best way you know how. We don't need anything coming back to trace us. Do you understand these instructions?" Kristian asks. "Yes" Lamar replies. "Good" Kristian says. The phone then hangs up. Lamar then proceeds with the steps that Kristian has set out for him.

"THE BRIDGE"

Lamar is at the Garden Bridge; this is the last part of his assignment that Kristian has instructed him to do. "With two ten pound weights in his bag, it should sink down to the bottom without a problem." He thinks to himself as he walks over to the guardrail of the bridge. He stops abruptly as he is about to throw the bag over the edge. He senses that he is being watched, but he can't pin point where it's coming from. So he pretends like he is marveling at the view of the monumental structures throughout the city. He then turns to his right and proceeds to walk to the other side of the bridge. The feeling of being watched seems to approach him even more closely. Lamar then looks further down the walkway of the bridge. He notices that a mysterious being in a hooded robe is walking towards him amongst the crowd of people walking along the way. As he and the mysterious person walk toward one another, He secretly slides out one of his blades and prepares for a confrontation, but as the two get closer, the mysterious being turns and hops over the edge of the bridge. While everyone is in shock of what has just occurred, Lamar keeps walking as if he is paying it no mind. As he passes the spot where the mysterious being leaped, he looks over the guardrail of the bridge and notices that there are no ripples in the water. "That wasn't just another suicide maniac." He says to himself.

Lamar tries to remember some of the characteristics about the mysterious being. From the way he or she walked and moved, he couldn't go by anything else sense the mysterious character was covered fully in a hooded robe covering his or her entire figure.

Lamar proceeds to another location to dump the evidence that can trace the job he has just completed back to him. He looks at his watch and notices that he has less than an hour to get to the airport. He scavenges around to find a place that no one will look. As he gets closer to a shuttle stop, he sees an old sewage drain. "This is the perfect place to dump it." He thinks to himself. As he gets closer to the location he looks around to make sure no one is watching him. Once he notices no one is, he moves quickly. "Splash" the bag sinks to the bottom of the sewage drain.

"IN FLIGHT"

The sound of air passing by the wings of the aircraft traveling in flight sets off the scene. Inside the gliding object Lamar sits back with his eyes closed. From the looks of his actions now, it's almost as if nothing has occurred. He feels calm and relaxed, but there's one thing he can't get out his head. "I wonder who it was?" He thinks to himself. He slightly remembers distinctively how the hands of the individual who leaped from the bridge looked. "They looked feminine," He thinks to himself. He also remembers seeing a tattoo or possibly a birthmark on the edge of the right hand. He feels that he has seen those hands before. He gets the feeling that the mysterious person is a woman that he has encountered before somewhere, but he just can't remember when.

"BACK AT THE LODGE"

A car pulls up outside the compound. Inside the chauffer looks back at Lamar and says "Goodnight". Lamar doesn't reply back, he just steps out the car and grabs his bag. He approaches the front door of the compound. He puts his hand on the doorknob, but before he turns the knob, he rests his forehead against the door and takes a deep breath and sighs out. He then opens the door and walks through. He walks with a fast pace throughout the place. He moves on about without saying anything to anybody. Then out of nowhere, he sees a distinctive looking hand as he is walking about. On the hand is a tattoo that is similar to the tattoo of the hand of the mysterious being on the bridge. He looks back, but whomever the tattooed hand belongs to is gone. Lamar stands in the hall of the busy compound and tries to sift through the crowd of the fellow assassins, but he doesn't have any luck. He then feels a funny feeling he has never experienced before, but he seems to be enjoying it. He then notices he is showing some form of emotion that is not allowed and quickly dismisses them. He proceeds to make his way to his room. As he pulls out his key, and sticks it in the keyhole. He stops for a short second. Thinking he may have heard something, he pauses and wonders if it's Kristian waiting on him to give him a report. He then proceeds to open the door.

"THROUGH THE DOOR"

As Lamar opens the door and walks into the dark room, a hand filled with softness suddenly pulls him in abruptly. As this happens he gets flipped onto his back. He looks up only to see a shadowy figure run out the dark room and into the hall filled with light. He then hops up quickly to his feet, running over to the light switch in his room and flicking it on. He looks around to see if there is anyone else in the room. He steps out into the hall and looks around, but he doesn't see who it was that has just confronted him. He then shuts the door and rests his back against it with his head looking up at the ceiling. He thinks to himself, "I haven't been knocked around like that since training." Suddenly there's a knock at the door. He already knows who it is. He opens the door. "Have you gotten any rest?" Kristian asks. "I just got in" Lamar responds. "Hmm, you seem to be stressed. Is there something on your mind?" Kristian says. Lamar hesitates and then answers "No" "Are you sure?" Kristian asks. "Yes" Lamar answers. "Well kid, the time has come." Kristian says. "What do you mean?" Lamar asks. "You'll soon find out on your next mission. Get plenty of rest tonight. You'll need it for your training tomorrow." Kristian says as he leaves out.

"TRAINING"

I t's the next morning and the sun is breaking through the clouds brightly. A ray of light hits Lamar in the face causing him to awake. He stands to his feet and walks over toward the window he so dearly loves to stare out. He does his routine stare over the scenery of the mountainous forest. It seems like the day is perfect whenever he stares at the amazing vista. He continues to stare only to look toward his left and noticing someone training in the field with what seems to be a staff of some kind of rod. He then looks closer and notices it's a female. Her beauty amazes him. "She's" thoughts race through his mind of the right words for him to think of. He finally settles on "She's beautiful!" he says to himself. Then out of nowhere that strange feeling comes back and travels throughout his body. While He is experiencing this emotion a knock at the door interrupts him. He then turns his attention to the door. He already knows who's on the other side. He opens the door. "I see you're enjoying the view!" Kristian says. Lamar thinks to himself "How?" "That's not important right now. You are looking at your new training partner. She will help you prepare for your next mission. Now don't get too excited kid, she is not to be taken lightly, so keep it professional." Kristian explains. "Get dressed and be down stairs in the next hour." He says as he leaves out and shuts the door behind him. Lamar looks out the window again only to see the beautiful female he is admiring, staring back at him. He admires her features. Her skin tone possibly that of a mixed race, jet-black hair, with the front of her hair somewhat curled to the side. The unknown woman turns around and walks away. He watches her until she's no longer in view.

Water running rapidly, the scene of the bathroom filled with steam. Inside the shower stands Lamar with his head resting against the wall under the water.

Lamar pulls his shirt over his head and puts on his over shirt. He then tightens his combat like degree black belt around his waist.

"AT THE DOJO"

Lamar makes his way into the dojo training area where Kristian and the mysterious woman await him. "You're early as usual! Hopefully you'll be early tomorrow." Kristian shouts out. Lamar approaches Kristian and the unknown female. Kristian then speaks. "This is Alina. She will help prepare you for your next mission. Don't get too excited, she's tougher than she looks." Lamar is listening but somehow Kristian's words become tuned out as he stares at Alina who is staring directly back at him. The look on her face is calm but intense. Lamar has no idea of what he is in for. She somewhat smirks at him to throw him off. He smirks back. She now knows that she has him.

"TRAINING BEGINS"

The training starts off intense and brutal. Lamar and Alina attempt to strike one another with the staff batons made of bamboo. Click, clack, click, clack, click, clack, sounds of the sticks colliding with one another. Thoughts are racing through Lamar's head. "She is relentless." He thinks to himself. Alina becomes increasingly aggressive with every strike and hit. She does a vertical leap and swings the stick with tremendous force, but Lamar manages to block the attack. As the training proceeds, Lamar is very much on the defensive while Alina is not letting up on her intensity. With every strike she breathes and hisses out loudly. Lamar is wondering when she will let up, but from the looks of things, she will not anytime soon. Lamar then decides to increase his intensity level. He then begins to take a more offensive approach. He strikes back at her with brute strength. She knows she has him where she wants him. Lamar then swings toward her head. She ducks down and makes her move. She spins around with the stick all while taking Lamar's legs out from under him. He falls on his back. She then swings the stick with tremendous force toward Lamar's face. "Huh!" she yells out, but Lamar manages to block the attack by putting his stick up. Clack, the sound that comes from the staffs colliding. There's a long pause in the room before Kristian says, "I told you kid, she's tougher than she looks!" Kristian says. Alina then steps back while Lamar hops back to his feet. He feels somewhat embarrassed, but he knows he can take her, so he lets her be the aggressor. He goes back on the defensive. They get back into their combat stance. Kristian yells out "Continue!" Immediately the sticks begin to collide. Lamar notices Alina aggressiveness has intensified. "She has plenty fire in her." He says to himself. Alina continues to be the aggressor. Lamar stays on the defensive and spots his opening. As soon as Alina lifts her stick up for a vertical strike down onto Lamar. He puts his stick out in a vertical position to block the attack. As the sticks make contact, Lamar spins his weapon in a circular motion, causing Alina to almost lose grip on her staff. As she tries to regain her firm hold on her weapon, Lamar takes out her legs, with a swift sweep. She falls onto her back, but she quickly hops back to her feet and tries to surprise Lamar with a quick strike to his ribs. She catches him. Lamar drops to one knee and looks up at her in shock. She then stares back at him and waits for a response from his facial expression, but he lets her know that she does not intimidate him. He stands up straight and looks into her in the eye and smiles. Alina then knows she is not dealing with a regular trainee. She says to herself "Time to turn it up a notch." She attacks with brute force. Her strikes are accurate, this time most of her strike attempts are successful, but Lamar doesn't let it phase him, though the hits to his body began to dwell on him, but he doesn't let it show. Click clack, click clack. The sounds repeat throughout the dojo. As time goes on he notices a pattern of the moves that Alina is executing. He now has control of the situation. Every time she attempts to strike, Lamar counters with a defensive strike. She feels the pain from the hits, but she keeps going until Lamar counters with a defensive strike again, but this time he grabs her staff, and attempts to snatch it from her. Alina shouts out "Big mistake!" She leaps into the air and performs a roundhouse kick to Lamar. Her foot nails him on the side of his face and sends him to the matt. As Lamar is falling he notices Alina's stick swinging towards his face at a fast pace. He puts up his forearm to block the strike. As the stick makes contact with his forearm, it breaks in two. "That's enough!" Kristian yells out. The pain from the contact of the stick to Lamar's arm is excruciating, but he hides it from Kristian and Alina. He stands to his feet and stares into Alina's eyes. He smirks in a somewhat charming manner. She doesn't show any reaction to him. She just stares back at him breathing heavily through her nostrils. "A bit too much for you to handle?" Kristian asks. "I'm fine." Lamar replies. He tries to cover up the pain, but Kristian can easily see that he's hurting. "You better try to heal up quickly, because tomorrow it's going to be even more intense." Kristian says. "I'll handle it." Lamar responds. "What do you think Alina? Do you think he's capable?" Kristian asks. Alina then takes a long stare at Lamar. She smirks and then answers, "He seems to be up for the challenge." "We'll see. That's all for today, make sure you both get plenty of rest." Kristian says as he walks off. Alina stares at Lamar for what seems to be an eternity. He stares back clinching his fist trying to ignore the pain that has been inflicted upon him. She then turns to her left and walks toward the exit of the dojo training room. Lamar's eyes follow her. Her beauty mesmerizes him again, but he feels that she has many hidden secrets. He smiles to himself for one quick second and grabs his swollen forearm and holds it as he walks toward the exit and proceeds back to his room.

"LICKING THE WOUNDS"

Raining water runs from the shower hose onto Lamar's beaten and bruised body. The blood from the gash on his arm leaks down the side of his arm and onto his fingers. It drips to the shower floor and runs into the drain. As he puts his head back with his eyes closed, he rewinds the whole training session back through his head over and over again. "She's definitely something beyond the imagination." He says to himself. He then opens his eyes with his head still titled back and stares at the ceiling of the bathroom. Then he asks himself "how can someone so beautiful yet be so aggressive and direct with her actions?" He wonders, "Where did she come from? How did she get here?" Lamar's curiosity runs rapidly, but he remembers where he is. The Regime doesn't allow these types of thoughts to transpire, so he begins to block them out, but he still finds himself thinking about Alina.

A few moments later Lamar shuts off the running water. As he does this he listens to the sound of the water running down the drain. He then steps out the shower stall and grabs a towel. He walks over toward the mirror and wipes away the misty steam on it. He proceeds to dry himself off. He then puts the towel over his head and dries his head. As he removes the towel from his face, he begins to stare at himself. As he examines his face, he notices a bruise on his right cheek. He feels soreness and stress coming from it as if he had just been struck by something. Then he remembers the roundhouse kick that was delivered to his face from the foot of Alina. He rubs his hand across his sore cheek and smiles at the mark she has left on him. "She thinks she's got me figured out, but I have something in store for her tomorrow." He says to himself. He turns to his right and proceeds to his bedroom.

Having taped up his sore forearm, Lamar is now prepared to rest up for the continuation of his intense training that he is due in for in the morning, but before he goes to lies down, he does his ritual stare out the window onto the beautiful landscape. The view seems to be even more beautiful at night as the moon sits high and shines brightly throughout the dark blue sky. He then walks over to his bed climbs in and pulls the comforter over himself.

"IN MY SLEEP AGAIN"

Flashes of Alina's face constantly appear. Lamar has visions of her training and preparing. Then suddenly she appears before him, but this time it's face to face. Her beauty intrigues him. She stares at him for a while, then she attempts to be going in for a kiss, but suddenly the vision is broken. A hard object swipes across his face. "Smack" The impact from the blow wakes him from his sleep abruptly. As he tries to get up, he finds himself at a disadvantage due to whoever it is behind the sneak attack is now face to face with him. As he is forced to lie on his back his attacker appears in front of him with a hooded robe on. The mysterious person armed with a staff, has it pressed against his throat region. He tries to get a clean look at the mysterious individual, but he sees nothing but darkness. The assailant then moves his or her head closer to Lamar's face, but still no sight of who it is. The assailant softly speaks "Trust". Then suddenly the mysterious individual jumps up with the staff still pressed against Lamar's throat. Lamar looks over to his left and notices that the window he usually stares out from every night is open. The mysterious person then leaves in a flash by quickly jumping from the bed to the floor and out the window. Lamar quickly gets up and runs over to the window to see where the mysterious person could have landed, but as he stares out the window he sees only darkness on the grassy ground below. He looks around the room, but nothing unusual appears. He then takes a deep breath and sighs, almost as if he is relieved that the situation is over. He closes the window and securely locks it. He walks back over to his bed and slowly gets under the comforter. While doing so he rubs the area of his face that was smacked. As he rubs the area he is reminded of the training he experienced earlier with Alina. He then begins to wonder. "Is it? It can't be!" he says to himself. He tries to go back to sleep, but he can't get the thoughts of who it could be in the hooded robe, but he has an idea of who it may be. He closes his eyes and begins to slowly go back to sleep.

"IMAGINE"

Lamar appears in a steamy bathroom. The scent that he smells within the air is that of jasmine. The smell intrigues him as he walks through the steam filled room. As he walks he hears the sound of running shower water spraying. He continues to find his way through the steam clouds. He then notices the frame of a female figure in the shower behind a glass door. As he gets closer he begins to notice the detail characteristics of the female. The first thing he notices is the jet-black hair of the individual. It appears to be soaked and sleek. He stares in awe at the beauty before him. Then suddenly the female turns around. Lamar stares back at her face until he notices that it's Alina. She stares back at him as if she knew he was there all along. Lamar opens the glass door and walks in the vicinity. He walks over toward her and gets close. He places his arms around her. They both lean in toward one another. As they begin to kiss, suddenly Lamar's eyes open. He looks over toward the window on his left and sees that it's morning. "Time to get up" He thinks to himself.

"TRAINING DAY TWO"

Lamar is up early as usual, but this time he's dressed in a quick fashion. He is anxious for what lies ahead today. He notices he has extra needed time. He spends the spare time peacefully. As he stretches he feels the stress from last night leaving his mind and body. He is now ready for the events to come later in the day. He soon hears a knock at the door. He opens it expecting for it to be Kristian on the other end, but instead he is surprised by the presence of Alina. There's a long pause between the two before Alina speaks. "You look ready, hope you bring your A game, because today I won't be holding back." She says. He smirks and replies, "I anticipate it." Alina smiles and walks away. Lamar then thinks, "She doesn't know what she's in for today." As Alina walks off smiling through the crowd of students in the hallway, she says to her self "He's still a bit green."

Lamar enters the dojo slowly. Kristian is waiting in his usual calm demeanor with his arms crossed starring toward the ceiling. Meanwhile Alina is stretching. Lamar walks along nonchalantly. As he's walking he examines Alina's physical features. She has on a full-fledged body suite that's all black. Meanwhile he takes a look at how well her form looks while she's in a Chinese split. She then leans forward and stretches out. Her form intrigues him. As he stares on, she lifts her head up and smirks at him in a flirtatious manner. Then suddenly Kristian yells out "Are you ready!" Lamar snaps out of his Trans and replies "Of course." "Good" Kristian says. "Today's training is going to be very intense. You two will be going to complete a mission together. I want you to develop trust with one another. That way you will be able to execute accurately." Kristian explains. "What do you mean together? I thought we worked alone." Lamar says. "No questions kid. You'll find out the rest when it's time for you to know. You'll need a change of clothes son, there's a set in the locker room waiting for you. Go change." Kristian demands.

"ATTIRE ADJUSTMENT"

Lamar walks to the locker room section of the dojo. He sees the attire that's set out for him, a set of all black combat gear. He picks up the clothes and walks to the very back of the locker room restroom area. Making his way from the restroom area is Valentine. Considered to be the Regime's second best assassin throughout their history after Kristian. He has been known to take out rooms of thirty targets or more at a time within an instant. Lamar walks by casually and speaks. "Valentine" he says as he greets him. "Don't be green kid, remember to control your desires and watch your hands!" Valentine says as he continues walking. Lamar turns around wondering what Valentine means by his statement. Lamar continues on his way to the back. As he walks into the restroom area he tries to figure out what Valentine is implicating. "Don't be green? What does he mean by that?" He repeats to himself. Lamar thinks long and hard about the statement. "And what does he mean by watch your hands?" He thinks. He tries to erase it from his thoughts, but it sticks in the back of his mind. He changes his clothes and takes a look in the full body mirror. He then smiles at the thought of Alina's beauty. He turns and proceeds to exit the restroom and locker room area to get back to the dojo to meet with Kristian and Alina.

"DEVELOPING CHEMISTRY"

"Pop,pop,pop,pop". Is the sound coming from the chamber of a mechanical sniper rifle firing off projectiles in an attempt to hit both Lamar and Alina. The cold wind is blowing so hard that Lamar can feel the sharpness of it in his bones, but he's experienced these conditions many times before. They move through the routine training fairly quickly. As they move about, Lamar is impressed with Alina's accurate and quick maneuvers throughout the course of the obstacles placed in front of them. As they make their way to the end, he notices that Alina is not aware of the last part of the course or so he thinks. The two of them make their way across a loose ladder suspension bridge made of rope and wood. As they approach the middle section of the bridge, the entrance part snaps, causing that side to collapse. As the bridge begins to fall on one side, Lamar and Alina both dive and grab hold of what they can. Once the bridge swings over and reaches the other side. They begin to quickly climb up. Within seconds they make it to the top. Lamar is first to make it. He turns back and extends his hand to help Alina. She looks up and stares him in the face and smiles. Then suddenly she slaps his hand away and pulls herself up. As this happens, Kristian who's watching the surveillance footage of the two begins to smile.

Lamar and Alina make it back to the training compound. They don't say anything to one another. They keep walking in a straightforward direction side by side. Lamar begins to think to himself. "What's on her mind?" As they proceed back to the compound.

"BACK AT THE POST"

Lamar and Alina finally make it back. Once they get there, Kristian is waiting for them to arrive. He greets them "Well you two seem to be getting along great. Nice attempt for the save Lamar!" Kristian says jokingly. Lamar replies as he turns and stares at Alina. "I help when I can." Alina with her arms crossed swings her hair over her shoulder and turns her head in the direction to where Lamar is standing "Not everybody is in need of assistance." She says. Lamar stares back at her and smirks. Kristian interrupts the tension between the two. "Well the chemistry between you two seems to be heating up on high. Never mind that, tomorrow you'll be off to carry out your mission. I want everything to be perfect. No mistakes, no flaws. Keep it clean and untraceable." Kristian explains. "What is it we're going to be doing?" Lamar thinks to himself. Kristian interrupts his thought by saying "No questions. I'll brief you the info tomorrow. Get plenty of rest tonight. You're going to need it."

"TIME FOR REST"

Lamar is once again performing his normal routine, preparing for a good night's rest. He looks at the beautiful night sky. He continues to wonder what type of mission he is being prepared for. He recalls the training that he and Alina just went through. He remembers specifically the part when the bridge made of rope and wooden slacks collapsed. He also recalls when he extended his hand out and she slapped it away. As he replays the situation back to himself slowly, he notices a tattoo at the end of her hand. He begins to think. "Could she?" he asks himself in a surprising manner. Suddenly there's a knock at the door. He pretty much knows who it is, so he walks to the door in a calm manner expecting some words of wisdom from Kristian. He opens the door, but to his surprise it's not Kristian, instead it's Alina. She starring at him with her arms crossed. Lamar makes a subliminal comment "You making another late night visit?" He asks. "What do you mean?" she responds. "Nothing" He says. She smirks, tilts her head back, closes her eyes and bites her lip as she gathers her thoughts. She then opens her eyes and stares Lamar directly in the face and speaks "You will be just fine just as long as you stay out of my way. Make sure you understand this, the target is mine, no matter what Kristian tells you!" She says. Lamar's facial expression then changes to a more serious tone. "Well don't expect for me to lie down and just take your commands. If Kristian gives me the order, believe me I'm going to take it, no matter how you may feel about it!" He replies. She is impressed with his aggressive tone, but she doesn't show it. She shrugs her hair back over her shoulder and steps forward so that she's face to face with him and speaks. "We'll see won't we? You have no idea of what I'm capable of. You better hope your able walk away from whatever happens tomorrow!" She says. Lamar smirks back at her and says, "I pretty much plan on it." They stare into each other's eyes for what seems like minutes. "Am I interrupting anything?" Kristian says as he cuts the tension between the two again. Alina Gathers her self and steps back. Lamar then speaks "No, we're just discussing certain events that went on earlier during training." Kristian smirks and responds "Are you sure? Cause I could leave you two alone." "We just had a little bit of a misunderstanding, but everything seems to be fine now, right Lamar?" Alina asks. Lamar turns to her and says, "I would hope so." Kristian then interrupts "Well I hope you two will be ready as can be in the next two days. Go rest up." Kristian walks off. Alina then makes a sarcastic comment. "Yes make sure you're well rested." She then walks off. Lamar smiles as his eyes begin to follow her as she continues down the hall. Her backside intrigues him as her bodysuit made of spandex is quite revealing. Alina can feel the energy of Lamar's eyes following her. She smiles graciously as she continues to walk down the empty hall. Lamar then closes his door.

"THE TASKMASTER"

Two days later, New York City. It's early and the air is very cold, windy and frigid. Lamar is walking at a brisk pace throughout the morning pedestrian traffic. He's focused on the task at hand. He makes it to the end of the corner of a busy intersection. Suddenly his cell phone rings. He stops and stares at the busy environment of pedestrians going on about their day as his phone continues to ring. He pulls the phone out and presses the answer key. He puts it up to his ear. "Took you long enough." Kristian says on the other end. "Just getting a feel for the environment" Lamar responds. Kristian then says "Well you're going to be short on time when it comes to that. I need you to make your way over to the warehouse district of the east river. Your target is located in what may seem to be an old rundown warehouse. Now I want you to be aware that this is no ordinary warehouse. There's a top of the line security force inside. Alina has already made her way there. She will give you a helping hand in taking out particular obstacles that may get in your way. Look to the building across from the warehouse, there is a dumpster around back. In there is where you'll find what's needed to complete this mission. Remember be aware of everything around you." Kristian says as he hangs up the phone. Lamar follows the instructions that were just given to him. As he walks rapidly through the crowded streets he prepares himself mentally. He flags down a taxi and gets in the back. He tells the driver where to take him. The taxi pulls off. The cab comes to a stop not far away from the river. Lamar pays the driver and steps out. As the taxi pulls off, Lamar turns east and begins to walk. The scene is quiet and empty. All he hears is his soft footsteps tapping the ground. He then approaches the building across from the warehouse. He walks up to the dumpster and opens the side door. Inside he notices a gym bag strap peaking through the many plastic trash bags. He pulls the bag out and opens it. As he examines what's inside, he notices a cell phone. He picks it up and turns it on. Suddenly a text message shows with a picture. He presses the view button. The text shows a picture of his target. "A slim face." Lamar says to himself. The man in the picture is a white male; possibly in his mid forties, slim build, with most of his facial hair shaved except for his mustache. Lamar examines the picture with great detail. He looks in the bag and notices an earpiece and microphone hook up. He takes it out and hooks it up to right ear. Once he hooks it up he tests it. "Testing, testing is anyone there?" He says as he speaks into the microphone. "I'm here." A soft voice comes through on his headset. "Who's is this?" Lamar asks as if he's clueless to who it is. "There's no need for guessing games, lets focus on the task at hand." Alina says. Lamar smirks and then asks "Are you in position?" Alina cracks a tiny smile. "If I wasn't then you would've already have been exposed yourself by now." She says. "What?" Lamar asks. She sighs and then says. "Take a closer look at the entrance." Lamar peaks around the corner and looks at the double door entrance in front of the building. He sees two security enforcers lying face down on their stomachs. "Well there goes the grand entrance." He says. Alina cracks a smile and then says, "Alright enough of the small talk lets finish the task." Lamar concurs and begins to move toward the building when he suddenly notices a red beam flashing in the crack of the double doors. He stops and examines. He notices that the front door entrance is rigged to blow. He moves over to the rusted down car in front of the building that is perpendicular to the building his target is supposedly located. He peaks around and starts to move toward the building. Then suddenly four gunmen on the third floor begin to shoot through the windows with rapid gunfire from their machine guns. Lamar quickly dodges the projectiles and makes it to the right side of the building. The gunmen now see that Lamar is out their range of view, but it's too late for them now. Alina has them all lined up for termination. "Clack clack clack clack". Her high-powered rifle takes them out with no problem. "You're clear." She tells Lamar. Lamar has to find a new way to gain entry into the building, but from the looks of things it seems impossible. He walks around to the back. "You're out of range," Alina warns him. "I can take care of myself" he responds. He peaks around and checks out the back. There's nothing in sight, but the flowing east river and a small crawlspace. He knows that whosever inside is expecting him, but he goes on about his way trying to find a way in. Meanwhile Alina breaks down the original rifle she has and pulls out parts to another. She quickly assembles it together. The rifle she has just assembled is more advanced. The scope on it has X ray vision allowing her to see inside the structure of the building. She turns up the calibration level. She quickly spots the target inside, but she doesn't pull the trigger. She's anticipating the moment for when she'll disappoint Lamar. She'll wait all day and night if she has to.

Around back Lamar finally finds a way inside the eight-story building. He spots a small ventilation shaft big enough for him to fit in. Only problem he has is that it's between the first and second floor. "If the target is possibly on the upper floor, there will be a lot of security to get by." He says to himself. He quickly climbs up to the ventilation shaft. He pulls out a small compact knife and begins to unscrew the screws to loosen the cover. He removes the cover and gently places it to the side carefully and quietly. He then begins to make his way into the crawlspace.

"ON THE INSIDE"

Lamar makes it to the other end of the crawlspace. He peaks through the vent cover in front of him. He notices a guard standing right below him armed with an SMG assault rifle. Lamar now knows that whoever his target inside is anticipating him. "I have to do this quietly or everything will be jeopardized." He says to himself. He makes contact with Alina. "I'm inside" He tells her. She smirks "I know your location already. The floor you're on is pretty much empty. There are only two guards there. One right in front of you and another pacing near the front window area." She tells him. "How does she know all of this?" He thinks to himself. "You're probably wondering how I know all of this. Well lets just say I'm armed with unique weaponry," She says. Lamar doesn't say anything in response. He is now ready to make his move. He gently presses his hands against the ventilation duct cover. Then suddenly he charges forward. Within an instant He charges from the crawlspace with knife in hand. The enforcer attempts to react, but he is too slow. Lamar is face to face with him, with the blade from his knife impelled in the enforcer's throat. Lamar covers the enforcer's mouth while looking around to analyze the scene. "It's quiet."

He says to himself. He slides the guard's body down the wall into a sitting position. "I'm in. The first enforcer has been taken care of." He says to Alina through his microphone attached to his earpiece. "The second one is out as well." She responds revealing that she has eliminated the second one. "Have you spotted the target?" he asks. "No, but my guess would be is that he is located on the upper levels of the facility. Kristian will send you a layout of the place." She tells him. Lamar confirms, and then asks, "What is security looking like on upper levels?" "Come on now, that's taking all of the fun out of it." She says. "Well I guess it won't be too much of a problem." He responds. He then proceeds onto the upper levels.

Lamar makes his way up to the third floor. The site of it would be unreal to most, but Lamar always expects uniqueness in every mission. As he makes his way undetected to the center of the fortress he is amused by the layout of the structure. It is similar to that of the Pantheon in Rome with an open center that leads all the way down to the first floor. The place is covered with armed gunmen patrolling the track like floors that circle around the interior. Lamar finds a good place to lay low until he receives the layout of the structure from Kristian. He makes contact with Alina. "I'm on the third floor." He says. "Okay have you received the info from Kristian?" She asks. "Not yet." He responds. "Well hold your position until he contacts you." She tells him. Lamar sits back and waits for the info.

"MOMENTS LATER"

Moments later Lamar receives a message from Kristian. He now has the entire layout of the interior. He notices that the area, in which he is located, is near the main lobby. There are plenty of long hallways with many rooms attached. Lamar thinks to himself. "The target could be in anyone of these areas." The layout of the place seems almost limitless, but Lamar knows that there is a way. "I just have to figure out a way to draw him out." He says. He scans around and notices the two double doors that seem to be the main entry to the second floor. "That's it," he says. He then goes into the hall that he entered the third floor through. He works his way down the stairwell quietly, but suddenly he encounters a guard making his way up. They bump into one another, but Lamar reacts quickly and grabs the guard by his head and snaps his neck. He lays the enforcer's motionless body down slowly on the steps. He then proceeds to make his way down the stair well. Once he reaches the second floor, he peaks his head around the corner. He notices there are two guards in the hallway leading down to the double doors. They're both heavily armed, but their weapons will not matter. The two guards cross one another's path, as one of them walks toward the entrance; the other makes his way toward the other end of the hall. Lamar moves quickly behind the one near the entrance and pulls out a small blade. Within an instant he disables the guard. He then turns his attention to the other guard who hasn't heard nor noticed what is going on. Lamar once again moves quickly and quietly as he takes out the second guard. Though he knows it's too late to check now, Lamar scans the hall looking for surveillance cameras, but there isn't any in site. He walks back over toward the stairwell and grabs the bag he brought with him. He creeps over to the double doors. He peaks through one of the small windows to see what is taking place on the other side. The guards are moving on about their regular routines. He then opens the bag and reaches in. He pulls out a magnetic electronic explosive device. He assembles it together quickly. He then plants the device between the two double doors. He turns the device on, and sets a timer for forty seconds. He activates it. The timer begins to countdown. Lamar turns away and quickly begins to move down toward the other end of the hall. He looks down at his wristwatch that's synced up with the timer on the device. As he waits for the right time, he pulls out two nine-millimeter pistols. The guards on the other side of the door have on their flack jackets and bulletproof vest, but he is not looking to hit any of them in the torso region. The timer and the watch continue to countdown 15, 14, 13, 12, 11 Lamar sets his feet. As soon as the watch strikes 8, he takes off. 7, 6, 5, 4, 3, 2, 1, an explosion goes off. As the flames spread over what was once the double doors; Lamar dives head first through them. As he reaches the other side he summersaults through and lands on the balcony railing with perfect balance. He takes a look at the scene. The guards have their guns drawn. Lamar then leaps forward in a diving motion with his arms extended outward with pistols in hand. The guards fire off many rounds, but none of their projectiles manage to touch him. He takes aim at the guards and shoots. He manages to take out four guards with headshots. Meanwhile Alina fires her high tech rifle through the walls of the structure and takes out a number of guards herself. As Lamar descends down to the base of the structure, he continues to fire off rounds. He manages to terminate many of the enforcers, but there are still plenty of them left. He flips forward and manages to land on his feet and down to one knee. He raises his head with a fierce stare in his eyes. The guards here are a lot more equipped and armored. "Stop!" one of the yells out. "Drop your weapons!" The guard says. Lamar still with great intensity in his eyes drops his pistols to the floor. He then puts his hands up and stands to his feet. The guards and Lamar stand off for a few seconds. Then one of them speaks out. "Everyone hold your fire!" A voice from the top floor of the structure breaks through. "Search and restrain him. Then bring him to me!" The male voice says. The guards do as they are told. They restrain Lamar and escort him upstairs to the eighth floor. Once they've reached the top of the structure, out steps the man who is in power. "Slim face" Lamar thinks to himself. It's the same man from the picture. He's dressed in a navy blue suit, without a tie. He walks over toward a restraint Lamar and says. "I know who sent you!" He says. There's a long pause after he makes his statement. "So they really feel like I'm a threat to the status quo? Well they've made their move, now I'll make mine; starting with you." He says. He moves closer in front of Lamar. "Put him on his knees!" He tells his men. They do as he says. Lamar waits for the right opportunity to arrive. The target then points to the table that the guards have placed Lamar's weapons on. One of the enforcers walks over to the table and picks up one of the many blades Lamar was armed with. He then walks over and hands it to the target. As he receives the blade, he examines it. "I wonder how many have you eliminated with these. Do you even know why you were sent here to kill me?" He asks. Lamar remains silent as he sternly stares into the eyes of his target. "Hmm, not much a talker are you? Well maybe this will cause you to react verbally." The target says as he moves closer to Lamar. He takes the blade and prepares to assault Lamar with it. The target motions his right hand back while holding the knife in hand. "Now" Lamar thinks to himself. He hops to his feet and slings the enforcer on his right side in front of the target just as his arm is swinging down with the blade in hand. The target impales his own enforcer in the shoulder and neck region. The enforcer screams out in agony. The enforcer on Lamar's left shoulder tries to restrain him by himself, but he's too slow and weak. Lamar uses that back of his head to head butt the enforcer in his nose region. The enforcer drops to his knees from the impact. Lamar kicks him in the chest, cracking his rib cage. The rest of the guards in the room aim their weapons and begin to fire. Lamar dodges many bullets and picks up the enforcer who he has just disabled SMG assault rifle and begins to let off shots. He takes out a few guards. Then He makes his way to the table and picks up his weapons. He drops the assault rifle and begins to throw some of his knives. He hits one of the guards in the wrist causing him to shoot wildly and take out some of his own comrades. Lamar grabs his target and throws him against the wall. "Go ahead." The man says. Lamar pauses at the thought of what the target has just said. Within an instant a hole appears in the man's chest. As blood squirts from the wound, Lamar thinks to himself. "What?" He releases his grip on the man. Alina then comes through on the headset. "You got a lot of company coming your way. I suggest you get out of there." She says. Lamar looks around and notices the huge number of guards heading his way. He looks around to find an exit, but the obvious way out is through the huge plate glass window. "Flush him out!" One of the guards yells out. A few of the guards throw in a few concussion grenades. Lamar quickly covers his ears. They make a loud noise as they explode. The impact from the blast manages to crack the glass. Lamar looks around slightly disoriented, but still conscious. He grabs the rest of his weapons from the table, and waits for the rest of the guards to enter the room. "He's still standing, take him out this time!" One of the guards yells. This time they take pins out of their grenades, but this time they aren't concussion grenades. They throw them in. Lamar's eyes widen up. He makes a run for the window. The bombs go off as he crashes through the glass and free falls eight stories down into the cold frigid water of the East River. He splashes into the water. He comes up to the surface of the ice chilling water. He breathes in a huge gasp of oxygen from the cold air. As he exhales out heavily steamed, he looks around, but there is nothing but water and debris from the blast. He notices the longer that he's atop the flowing current chilling water. The water on his head begins to slowly turn into ice. He knows that if he stays in any longer he will freeze to death. He keeps moving around to keep his blood circulating. He swims inward toward land, but the walls of the canal are too high for him to reach. He gets close to the wall. Then suddenly "vroom" there's a boat approaching. It slows down as it slowly cruises closer to him, he looks to see who it is that is anchoring it. He notices black hair blowing in the wind. He then sees that it is Alina. As she pulls up she smiles. "Keeping yourself on ice for me?" She shouts. Lamar with a look of relief on his face rolls his eyes. She then helps him aboard. He's shaking rapidly and begins to clinch and breathe heavily. She puts the tarp used to cover the boat around him and wraps it. "Hang in there; you're going to be alright." She says.

"A WARM AWAKENING"

Lamar opens his eyes to a room that has a fluorescent orange like tone. He looks around the silent room. He knows that he is not back in his room at the compound. He rises to a sitting position, shifts his body to his right and plants his feet over the edge of the bed onto the floor. He notices that his clothing has been changed. He's only wearing a pair of pajama pants and no shirt. He rubs his hand over his left eye. He stands to his feet in a sore and stiff manner. He then proceeds to step forward, but as he continues to walk he begins to limp. He makes his way to the bathroom and flicks on the light switch. The brightness from the all white light makes him squint his eyes somewhat. He walks over toward the sink and turns on the faucet. He looks at himself in the mirror as the water runs. As he examines himself, he notices there's a full body mirror behind him. He notices that there are stitches on his shoulder blades. The one to the right side of his back is in a slightly slanted position, and the one on his left side is vertical. He slowly raises his arm and rubs the back of his head. There's a small lump from a knot. He knows that in time his wounds will heal. He looks back into the forefront image and stares himself in the face as the hot steam from the water begins to rise up and fog the mirror. He intakes a deep breathe and exhales out in a calm manner. He then leans over and splashes water onto his face with both hands and slowly rubs down to his chin. He raises his head up slowly and stares back into the mirror. Just as he does so, abruptly from nowhere Alina appears behind him. She then lifts up a pistol and puts it against the back of his head. "Don't move." She says. Lamar then asks, "What's this?" "You almost took my kill. Remember I told you that it was my kill not yours." She responds. Lamar stares back hard into the mirror in the reflection of her eyes. "It was my kill to begin with; you still managed get what you wanted. If you're not satisfied with it, then I suggest that you pull the trigger." He says. She's shocked by his response. She cracks a small smirk to the side. She then pulls the trigger. Click. Lamar stares into the mirror with no fear in eyes. He then turns around quickly and grabs her arms and pushes her against the wall. He moves in close to her. They both begin to breathe heavily. "Do you usually let off empty rounds?" He asks. "It depends on the situation." She responds in a sarcastic manner. He then begins to lean in toward her. "Well what kind of situation would you call this?" He asks. She then breathes out and inhales the intimacy and they begin to kiss. He then begins to remove her all black blouse. She then pushes him back against the sink and places her hands against his chest and rubs gently. He then begins to turn his attention toward her neck region and gently kisses her. She tilts her head back with her eyes closed and sighs. He knows from the reaction she's giving off that it has been a while for her. He then becomes a slight bit more aggressive. She wraps her arms around him and begins to hug him tightly. He places his arms around her and lifts her up by both her legs. They make their way to the bedroom. He lays her down gently onto the bed. She stares back and smiles. "What are you waiting for?" She asks. "Nothing." He responds. He then grabs her pants by the bottom and begins to slide them off slowly. She rises up and unties the drawstring on his pants and snatches them down to the floor along with his underwear. He pushes her back down to the bed. He reaches and proceeds to slide off her panties. He then gets atop of her and in between her legs. They aggressively kiss one another. Lamar slowly begins to enter inside her. While she quietly moans, he gently kisses her neck softly. As he begins to speed up the moans coming from Alina become somewhat louder and passionate. She bites his bottom lip and tries to hold it all in, but she eventually gives in and breathes out with a loud moan. Lamar quickly muffles her with a kiss. She then begins to smile and laugh. Then suddenly she grabs him by his shoulders aggressively and turns him over. Now the rolls are reversed, she is now in the dominant position. She leans down toward him and they begin to kiss more and more passionately with her hair spread across, covering her face somewhat. She then leans back and sits up straight and proceeds to move up and down, while whipping her hair back and inhaling deep breaths. She places her hands onto his chest to gain leverage. His reaction to her aggressiveness is calm but at times he stretches his head back while trying to fight off making a loud noise. She then leans her head back and climaxes. Not too long after he finishes as well. She grabs and grips his hands as she leans into him and kisses him gently with a light touch of aggression.

Moments later they lie together and cuddle. While she sleeps, he is still awake. He stares at the ceiling and thinks while he gently massages his hand on her shoulder. He then turns his head toward her and stares at her while she sleeps. He cracks a peaceful smile and turns back to stare at the ceiling. He breathes out as if the weight of the world has been lifted off his shoulders. He feels that he now knows what it may feel like to experience some form of love.

"THE NEXT MORNING"

Dim light from the cloudy sky beams through the blinds of the hotel room. Lamar wakes up in a cheerful mood. He feels relaxed. Only to discover he has waken up alone. He looks around and thinks to himself "Where is she?" Alina appears in the hallway leaning against the wall with a glass of water in hand. "Did you sleep comfortably?" She asks. He smirks "I slept good enough." He says. He notices that she is fully dressed as if she is prepared to leave. He then asks, "Going somewhere?" "I have to get back to the compound before Kristian suspects something is wrong. He'll probably be calling you in the next five minutes or so." She explains. She then slowly drinks the water down in one gulp. She slams the glass down on the table. "Don't be late, and don't mention a word about what has taken place. There's a lot going on that you don't know about." She says. Her statement makes him ask, "What do mean?" "In time you'll find out." She responds. She then turns and walks toward the door, opens it and stares back "And for the record, what happened yesterday was me taking matters into my own hands." She says. She then exits out and closes the door. Lamar with a look of confusion on his face begins to gather himself to leave. Suddenly the phone next to the bed begins to ring. He looks at it, reaches over and picks it up. A voice of German accent comes through "Having fun?" Kristian asks. Just as Alina said he would do. "What do you mean?" Lamar responds. Kristian laughs "Ha, ha, ha great job kid, you are definitely walking in my foot steps!" He says. Lamar is not flattered, he hears the subliminal tones behind Kristian's voice, he just can't pin point what it is. "Well kid time to come home and prepare for a new leaf. Your ticket is already set up for you at the airport. You know the routine." Kristian says. Lamar then confirms, but before they hang up "Hey don't take too long, your flight will be departing within the next two hours. Lamar's eyes cut to his right as if he is starring into the phone. "Fine" he says. The two hang up and proceed.

"ON THE WAY HOME"

Lamar is at the airport, LGA to be exact. He's at the ticket printout. He puts in the confirmation number that Kristian has sent him. The boarding pass prints out. He snatches it and walks away.

Lamar sits in his cozy seat amongst first class. He patiently waits to reach his destination. Meanwhile he closes his eyes and drifts into thoughts of his encounter with Alina not too long ago. He smiles at the thought of them kissing one another. He remembers vividly how beautiful her body is. He then recalls the details of her body. He recalls the tattoos on her arm. He thinks to himself. "I've seen that tattoo before." He sorts through his memories. Then suddenly he remembers "The Bridge!" He thinks to himself. He opens his eyes wide. "Hmm she's the one. What was she doing there?" he asks. He doesn't know what to think of the situation. "Is she spying on me for Kristian?" he thinks to himself. "I may not know what to think of it, but one thing is for certain, I know her and I will encounter one another again." He says to himself in his thoughts. He then lays his head back and breathes out peacefully.

"BACK AT THE LODGE"

It's the usual routine after a long flight back. The chauffer makes the long drive through the mountains and wilderness. They get to the compound and Lamar tips the driver. He steps out the car and with his bag in hand. He shuts the door and watches as the car drives off. He walks inside. The compound is not as busy as it usually is. There are a few people roaming around, but not many. As Lamar makes his way through the halls on his way to his room, he encounters Valentine. "Aww there's The Regime's bright future! How are you kid?" Valentine asks. Lamar can sense the sarcasm behinds Valentine's words, but he ignores it and says, "I'm good." "That's great kid; keep up the great work ethics!" Valentine says. He then walks off. Lamar gets to his room and opens the door, but before he walks in, he looks around as if he knows someone's presence is following him. He then proceeds to make his way into his room.

"IN MY SLEEP AGAIN"

Visions of Alina come across Lamar's mind as he sleeps. Memories of their last encounter with one another soothe his mind as he sleeps. Then he remembers what she said as she was exiting out the hotel room. "In time you'll find out." She says. He then abruptly awakes. He sits up, and pauses for a while as he gathers his thoughts. "Find out what?" He asks himself. "What is it that she could have been referring to?" He pauses again and remains silent while thinking. Then suddenly there's a knock at the door. Lamar knows who it is. He gets out the bed and walks over toward the door and opens it. "Ahh there he is!" Kristian says calmly. Lamar remains silent as usual. "Great job kid, you're definitely on the rise. Soon you'll be calling the shots around here if you keep up the progressive work." Kristian says. Lamar still remains silent. He continues to remain quiet as Kristian speaks. "Well kid it seems that you may need to take a vacation and enjoy yourself." He says. Lamar is surprised by Kristian's suggestion. "Vacation?" Lamar asks. Kristian with a sharp smile "Yes kid you've earned it." He says.

Lamar knows that there is more to it, but he remains silent. "I've already got the perfect place in mind." Kristian says and pauses at the thought of it. "I hear Monaco is real nice around this time of year!" He follows up with. Lamar then knows it's already time for another mission. "I've heard the same." Lamar responds. "That's the spirit now make sure you remember to have fun!" Kritian tells him. Lamar thinks to himself "This is unusual, him telling me to have fun; just doesn't make any sense." "When do I leave out?" Lamar asks. Krisitian responds "You know kid; you've got a great knack for asking the right questions. Ha ha, yes! There will be a car out side first thing in the morning around eight. Everything you're in need of will be available to you once you get there. Make sure you dress relaxed." Kristian then walks off "Rest up!" he says as he exits and closes the door behind him. After Kristian leaves, Lamar sits and thinks for a while. "Hmm Kristian is usually not this relaxed when it comes to missions. I wonder what's really going on." He pauses after his thought. Then the thought of Alina crosses his mind. "I wonder where she is?" he says to him self. He then flicks off the light switch and climbs back into bed.

"DREAM PARTY"

Las Vegas, Nevada, three years earlier, Lamar walks into a rich gallery filled with many people having a great time. There's music playing and people dancing. The gallery is dark with flashes of colorful lights flickering throughout. The music in the place is hype and up-tempo. As the party goes on Lamar is seen scouting out the scene from what seems to be a balcony or an overhead bridge where guest can oversee the view of the rich gathering. As he stares into the crowd, he recognizes his target. A Russian mob boss, who loves to make his appearance at highly exclusive parties and gatherings amongst the rich, little does he know that this will be his last. Lamar goes back through his steps of execution. He makes his way down to the dance level floor not far from where the mob boss is lounging. Behind him is a huge window with a view of a city that never sleeps. Lamar slowly reaches for his weapon of choice; a small compact thirty two caliber pistol that shoots accurately if the right area on the body is targeted, preferably the temple region of the head. Lamar stands back and waits for the right moment. He notices a waitress walking with an expensive bottle of champagne atop a trey with glasses. This is the perfect timing. Lamar knows if he aims correctly he can shoot through the bottle and nail his target all while making an exit without being noticed. As the waitress walks past the target Lamar thinks to him self "The window is open, here's your moment now!" Within an instant Lamar makes his move. He pulls out the small gun quickly and unnoticeably he pulls the trigger. A loud pop follows. The gallery fills with screams and horrific sounds. The mob boss falls back onto the sofa motionless. Lamar quickly makes his way through the panicky crowd and makes a quick exit just like he planned.

"BACK TO REALITY"

Lamar wakes up abruptly. The sun has just risen above the clouds. He knows it's still early, which means he has time to prepare for his trip. A few hours later an all black luxury car pulls up outside and the horn for it blows. The doors of the compound open and Lamar walks out and gets into the car and shuts the door. The car immediately pulls off. As they travel on their way to the airport, he sits back and thinks about Alina some more. "I wonder what's going on with her." He says to himself. He then shakes away the thoughts of her and says to himself. "I have to focus on the task at hand." He then sits back, relaxes and prepares himself mentally for what may be in store for him.

"WELCOME TO MONACO"

Sounds of aircraft coming and going roars throughout the scene; Lamar dressed in an all black suit makes his way through the pedestrian traffic. He keeps to himself and continues to walk as if no one is present.

"CHECKING INN"

Lamar gets to his hotel room. He opens the door and stares inside for a few seconds before stepping in. As he walks in he hits the light switch and looks around cautiously. He then walks over to the king sized bed and sits his bag on the floor while he takes a seat on the edge of the bed. He takes his right hand and rubs it against his head and breathes out. He begins to remember his last trip here just two years earlier. The Monte Carlo hotel and casino; just two years younger than he is now, Lamar waits in a room with sniper rifle in hand looking through the scope through a window that looks out onto the backside manicured lawn. He waits for his target to make his way throughout the yard. The target is a black male of Ugandan descent, possibly in his late thirties or early forties. He's dressed in a very expensive suit made by Versace. As the man walks casually in a peaceful manner, Lamar waits until the right moment to execute. As the man makes his way by the pool area, Lamar sees his window of opportunity. He pulls the trigger with a light touch. "Pooch" the projectile flies from the chamber of the rifle and immediately nails the target in the left temple of his head, forcing him to fall to his right side into the pool. The man's body smacks the surface of the water. Lamar sits back and observes his work. He watches, as the water in the pool turns red from the blood leaking from the skull of the deceased target. There's pandemonium throughout the place as some of the guest at the resort run over to see what the commotion is. Then some of the people who are present begin to point in the direction that Lamar is located. Once he notices this he quickly makes an exit from the room and escapes from it all.

Once the flash back is over, Lamar opens his eyes and breathes out with a sigh. He gets up and walks over to the bathroom. He hits the light switch and walks over to the sink, turns on the faucet and begins to wash his hands as he stares into the mirror. Suddenly flash backs of Alina come to mind. He smiles at the thought of their sexual encounter. He then cups his hands, closes his eyes, leans forward and splashes water onto his face. He slowly rubs his hands down his face while opening his eyes, but he realizes that this time no one is behind him. He then says to himself "One day." He then smiles and turns the faucet off.

It is a few hours later Lamar is lying across the bed with his eyes wide open starring at the ceiling. He lies there thinking, and then suddenly the phone next to the bed rings. He turns his head to the right, reaches over and takes the phone off the hook and puts it to his ear expecting to hear Kristian's voice. "Resting up?" but it's not the rough German accent of Kristian. Instead it's a soft voice to his surprise. It's none other than Alina. "Why are you calling me here?" He asks. "You don't have much time." She says. "There's an assault team heading to your room right now as we speak. You need to get out now." She tells him. Lamar with a look of confusion on his face then says, "What are you talking about?" He asks. "No questions just leave!" she says as she hangs up quickly. Lamar with the phone still to his ear hears a knock at the door. He puts the phone back on the hook slowly and quietly. He walks over to the door and looks through the peephole. On the other side of the door he sees there are at least five men heavily armed to the tee with high tech weaponry. He steps back cautiously. He knows that he doesn't have any weapons on him, he can only use what is at hand for him to use at the moment. The knocks at the door continue. He looks around to see if there's a place he can hide, but he has to do it quickly. Suddenly the door flies open almost as if a bolder was rammed against it. He quickly makes his way into the bathroom and quickly turns the lights off. He runs over to the shower and turns on the water. He then makes his way behind the door of the bathroom. Two of the five heavily armed men make their way over to the bathroom. They use hand signals almost as if they're in the military. Lamar notices an ice bucket on the shelf close by the door. He grabs it quickly before the two men make their way in. he waits patiently and quietly for the right moment to react. The two-armed men try to move slow and quietly, but Lamar can hear their every move. The first man enters in and the second one follows. Lamar sharpens his eyes and focuses in on when to attack. The two men then turn on their spotter lights that are connected to their assault rifles. The first of the two makes his way over to the shower and slides the shower door open. He aims in but he notices that no one is inside. He looks back at the other guy behind him with a surprised expression on his face. Lamar sees the perfect opportunity. He comes from behind the door and swiftly throws the ice bucket at the first enforcer near the shower. The bucket hits him across the bridge of his nose stunning him and sending him into a state of confusion. The second man turns around, but he's too late. Lamar quickly runs to him and disarms him of his weapon and disables him. He doesn't give the first enforcer anytime to recover. He immediately fires off three rounds. The enforcer falls down on his side. The other enforcers are alert. The third one runs in, but he is met with a surprise from a flying projectile to the face. He drops to his knees and then falls flat on his stomach. The last two enforcers begin yelling at one another in French. Lamar doesn't pay any attention to it, but he knows they are in fear for their life. They make their way to the left of the room near the full view window overlooking the resort with the pool below. Lamar checks the magazine of the rifle, he's got plenty rounds left, but he knows he has to find a quick way out, because there could be more enforcers in the hallway outside the room. He peaks out the bathroom from the corner and notices that one of the enforcers is a little too close to the window. He sees the perfect opportunity to make his move. He darts from around the corner of the bathroom full speed. He pulls the trigger on the assault rifle taking out the first enforcer in his path, while the second one tries to hit him with rounds from his assault rifle. But just like his comrade he's too slow. Lamar darts at him with full force and spears him through the glass window. As gravity pulls them both down seven floors, the enforcer yells in fear. Lamar with a calm demeanor waits until they hit the water of the pool. Both their bodies smack the surface of the water. Lamar uses the enforcer's body to cushion his fall somewhat, but he ends up hurting himself in the process. He's somewhat dazed from the impact, but he manages to swim up to the surface. He peaks his head up and breathes in heavily. He swims painfully over to the wall, while gritting his teeth to hold the pain in. He climbs out the pool, while spectators make their way over to help; he dismisses them and painfully limps away from the commotion. He makes his way into the lobby. As he walks to the exit, one of the lobbyists of the hotel tries to give him assistance. "Do you need help sir?" He asks. "No" Lamar says and pushes him away harmlessly. He limps outside to the front of the hotel entrance. He hunches over and puts his hands on his knees and tries to catch his breath. He looks up and looks around and notices a suspicious French man making his way over towards him. Lamar acts as if he doesn't notice him, but he's prepared to deal with him. As the man gets closer he reaches into his coat pocket for something. Lamar positions himself to counter act whatever it is that the man has planned. The man then removes his hand from his pocket and to Lamar's surprise he pulls out a set of keys. He walks over to the car that is parked directly in front of Lamar. The man opens the door, gets inside and starts the engine. The man puts his hands on the steering wheel and turns his head towards Lamar and stares at him while he's hunched over trying to gather himself. Lamar stares back wondering what it is that the man is thinking. Lamar then notices a reflection off the window. It's the lobbyist from a few moments ago. Lamar stands up straight and turns around quickly. The lobbyist walks up to him and says "Are you sure you don't need help sir?" While at the same time he pulls out a taser and prods Lamar in the stomach region with it. Lamar falls down to his knees then onto his side. He's unconscious. The perpetrator then quickly opens the back door of the sedan; grabs Lamar, lifts him up and places him in the backseat. The man then shuts the door and gets into the front seat while the car pulls off.

"FLIGHT INTERMISSION"

Lamar sits unconscious on a private military aircraft. He comes in and out of consciousness for a few seconds at a time. He hears voices of the two men who captured him. One of them says to the other "He's different from the other Regime marks that we have eliminated. He must've received advanced training." The other man responds "Couldn't have been that advanced, we still managed to capture him." Then there's a third distinctive voice that interrupts. "Enough of you two bragging, we have him now and soon we shall find the answers; administer him the injection so that he'll stay sleep throughout the flight." The man says. "That voice, it sounds vaguely familiar, but I can't..." Lamar thinks to himself all while receiving an injection of an unknown sleeping agent of some sort. As the drug is administered he fully loses his consciousness again.

"PAIN AND TORTURE"

Lamar wakes to the sound of water drops leaking from pipes of an underground like fortress or structure. He's dazed and confused. His vision slowly goes from blurry to clear. He sees nothing but a steel door in front of him with a barred up window, but no glass. He notices that he's strapped down to a chair. The room or cell is extremely moist and humid. He looks around, but sees nothing but rusty walls to his left and right. He notices at the top right corner within the room that there's a surveillance camera. He now knows that he is being watched. He leans his head back and breathes out. His head still aches from the seven-story fall. He notices that there's blood slowly running down the side of his face from a cut on the right side of his head. Then suddenly there's a click clack sound of the steel door being unlocked. The heavy door slowly opens. Lamar sits and anticipates whom it is that is going to walk in and to his surprise Valentine appears with a huge grin on his face. "Surprise, surprise kid." He says. Lamar doesn't say anything he just sits back and tries to observe what's going on. "You thought you were home free didn't you? I really liked how you took that seven-story fall. I just knew for sure that you were dead, but just like you feel right now, I was surprised to see you come out of that water." Valentine explains. Lamar is surprised for sure, but he's not going to let valentine know it. He smirks and says, "No, I'm not surprised, not at all." Valentine then smiles and asks "Why are you not surprised?" "I knew there was some sort of suspicion going on with you, I just couldn't quite figure it out." Lamar responds. "Hmm really! Well if you're not surprised now, then this will definitely surprise you. Come in!" Valentine yells out. Suddenly from behind Valentine through the doorway in comes Alina. Lamar tries his best to not look bothered, but it shows somewhat. She walks over to Valentine who wraps his arm around her and kisses her. Once they stop kissing, Valentine with an evil smirk on his face turns and stares at Lamar, but Alina puts her head down in what seems to be a shameful manner. Valentine then walks over to Lamar, hunches over and stares him in the face "Surprised now?" He asks. Lamar leans back in the chair and says nothing. Valentine then turns around and walks away. "Nothing shows a man's true colors like a woman!" he shouts. Lamar doesn't pay any attention to Valentine. He just stares sternly at Alina, but she can't look him in the eye. She turns her head away in guilt. Valentine continues talking. Then he says something that finally catches Lamar's attention. "Do you know what's going on?" Valentine asks. Lamar remains quiet and still says nothing. "Remember when we last bumped into one another? I told you not to be green, but you didn't listen" he says. Lamar then asks "Did Kristian put you up to this?" Valentine then laughs and says,

"No, do you seriously think that he is behind this? He's not smart enough. He's just an old man looking for salvation, but if there's one thing in this world that is not guaranteed, then that would be salvation!" Lamar then turns with a stern look on his face "So you're acting alone?" he asks. Valentine with his continuous grin "You know this is really not my style, but I guess every once in a while the truth needs to be shown to the blind." He says. He pauses for a moment. "No, I'm not acting alone, it's just when rules are broken, someone has to be disciplined!" He says. "Disciplined?" Lamar asks. "Yes kid, that last little job you did took the life of someone very important and dear!" Valentine explains. "Dear to whom, you?" Lamar asks. "No, he was a very important piece to the puzzle that holds this entire world together!" Valentine says. "I was doing what was asked of me, and as I recall I wasn't the one who terminated him." Lamar states as he stares at Alina. "Yes that may be true, but did you notice anything out of place during your so called job?" Valentine asks. Lamar then thinks to himself and remembers precisely what happened. Especially the little part where Alina terminated the target, he now knows that the whole mission was a set up. Lamar turns his attention to Alina and asks, "So the mission was a set up? And now I'm being blamed for it, but it was Kristian who gave me the mission to complete." Valentine quickly cuts off Lamar. "Yes you thought it was Kristian who gave you the mission, but I'm the one who manufactured it and switched the targets." Valentine explains. "You see kid, Alina and I are not exactly part of the Regime. We're simply pieces put in place to help maintain order." Valentine says. "Order from whom?" Lamar asks. "The Factions." Valentine answers. "Factions?" Lamar questions. "The six factions, you see the Regime is just a group of assassins and workers who take orders from the Six Factions. Whatever they order, The Regime has to follow." Valentine explains. "So was it them who put you up to this?" Lamar asks. "Not exactly, but in some ways yes. See the bosses have been watching Kristian for a long time now. We know he's up to something, we just can't pin point what it is. So I took the liberty of switching the targets on your last assignment. Kristian has been around for a long time. He practically knows everything about the Factions, but he refuses to join and leave The Regime in a set of new hands. He's left them in fear of what he might do next." Valentine explains. "I see where this is going, and I'm willing to bet the set of new hands that you are speaking of just so happen to be yours." Lamar says. "You know kid, you're bright. I'm slightly impressed by your assumption. I've been waiting fifteen long years to take over, and this will be my opportunity." Valentine says. "So this so called plan of yours is what you think may give you the power over the Regime?" Lamar asks. "Yes, perfect plan isn't it?" Valentine says. "It would be, except you have one little problem." Lamar says. "What's that?" Valentine asks. "They won't believe you." Lamar responds. "Well all the evidence that I've forged will make them believe me. All I have to do now is get any important information that I can gather from you along with getting rid of the only person who is part of the problem; that being you, and Kristian will fall. Let's say we see how long your tolerance for pain will last." Valentine says as he walks over to a table set up with various tools of torture. He picks up a lead pipe and says, "Shall we begin?" He walks over to Lamar and asks him, "Has Kristian by any chance given you a layout of his plan?" Lamar then stares back at Valentine and says, "Why should it matter? If you're going to kill me anyway?" Valentine then smiles and within an instant he takes a swift swing landing across Lamar's face with the pipe. "Well you can either give me any information that you have now and make this quick and painless or you can play the mute act and suffer a slow and painful demise." Valentine shouts. Lamar spits blood out from his mouth. He then looks up at Valentine and smiles. "Is that what you call suffering?" He asks. Valentine then smiles and says "You know kid; I'm going to enjoy this!" He takes another swing and then another. Lamar spits out more blood. He's somewhat dazed, but he's still functional. He takes more hits, but with each strike he becomes angrier. Valentine stops and drops the small lead pipe on the ground, and walks away. "You know it surprises me how much people in this world don't really know what's going on behind the many closed doors of our society that they pass by everyday." Valentine says. He then walks back over to the table to select a new tool. Lamar turns his attention to Alina and stares at her in a disappointed manner. She puts her head down in shame and stares at the floor. Meanwhile Valentine picks up a small blade. "You know the human body has many parts to it that are critical. They are very easy to find with just a swipe of a blade, but I'm pretty sure you already know this by now." Valentine says. Lamar remains quiet. He knows the pain is only temporary. As he anticipates what's coming his way, he looks at Alina again for a slight second. They make eye contact before she turns away and begins to walk out of the cell. She rubs her hand on Valentines shoulder and leaves out. Valentine smiles at her as she exits. He then transforms back into torment mode. He walks toward Lamar in a slow fashion. "You know when the Regime started up all those many years ago, they had class and decency, and now all of you just act like a pack of wild animals. Kristian and the rest of you dogs just think you can stand in the way of those who deserve to be in control. It seems as if there isn't any structure within the organization. That's why I will finish all of you off!" As Valentine finishes his statement, he takes a razor and swipes it across the side of Lamar's abdominal region. Lamar grits his teeth and begins to breathe heavily from the sharp pain sensation of the cut. Blood from the fresh wound begins to leak out like water. "Ha ha ha. You know why your blood is running like water right now? Well let me explain it to you so that you know just how it works. You see I cut just deep enough where your blood mixes with other fluids within your body. Fluids like puss, fat and last but not least water." Valentine explains as he makes several more cuts to the sides of Lamar's abdominal section. Lamar knows everything that Valentine is saying is just part of the psyche of torture, but he continues to wait until the right moment to make his move. As he sits strapped to the chair in agony. He slowly begins to fondle with the cuffs on his hands. He knows he can squeeze one of his hands free of restraint, but it will require him to possibly dislocate one of his thumbs. So he continues to wait until the right moment. Valentine walks back over to the table and picks up a small hammer. "Hmm you know kid I'm quite the handyman. You know what's ironic about this is back when the Regime first started up; it was nothing but a bunch of reject carpenters taking orders from the higher ups." Valentine explains. Lamar then sees an opportunity. "So is there a point to this sad story?" He asks Valentine in a sarcastic manner while grunting. Valentine is not pleased with his actions and he shows it in his tone of voice and posture as he walks over to Lamar. "The point is that you rejects need discipline, now tell me what has Kristian told you about his plans." As Valentine says this he swings the hammer down swiftly and strikes Lamar in his right quadriceps. Lamar hunches over in pain all while at the same time dislocating his thumb and squeezing his right hand free from one of the fasten cuffs freeing one of his arms, but he doesn't attempt to fully free himself just yet. He grabs his right thumb with his left hand and slowly snaps it back into place. He leans back in the chair and exhales out heavily trying to relieve himself of the pain. The pain from the strike to his right quad is ecstatic and he feels the pulse beating heavily in his thigh. He thinks to himself "It's bruised but not broken, once he walks back over to the table I'll have enough time to make my move." Valentine with a fierce grin on his face "You know the thing about animals is that they can be tamed. All it takes is some muscle, and a foot being put down." He says. He then slowly turns around and begins to stride back to the table. Lamar sees his opening like viewing sunlight through a freshly cleaned glass window. He moves his arm forward and leans down to untie his legs from the branded rope holding them together. He knows he has to do it quickly or he won't get another chance. He unties the rope, but leaves it wrapped around his ankles to make it seem as if he's still tied up. He then puts his arm back behind his back. Valentine sifts through the tools of torture and looks for the next one to use. He continues to hold the small hammer in his left hand. While he's doing this Alina has returned back to the cell. She looks over at Lamar and makes eye contact with him and winks with a sinister smile on her face. Valentine continues to search for his next weapon to utilize. He sits the hammer down and places both his hands on the table as if he's frustrated. Alina walks over to him and rubs her hand on his arm to comfort him. He looks over at her and grabs her by the back of her head and plants his lips against hers. Lamar becomes somewhat infuriated by their actions in front of him, but he keeps his anger in check and continues to wait until the right moment to make his move. As Valentine and Alina continue to kiss one another in what seems like forever, they abruptly stop with Valentine snatching her head back while he breathes out heavily. He then smiles in a sadistic manner. He releases his grip of her hair from his fingertips slowly. Lamar thinks to himself that now would be the perfect time to attack, but he knows he's out matched. He knows he may have the speed advantage, but Valentine has much more strength, plus with his sore leg; he won't be fast enough to react to Valentine's brute force. Valentine turns his attention back to the table and picks up a much larger hammer and a large size rusty nail used for chiseling. He turns around with a sinister smile on his face. "You see that's what it's all about kid. Brute force, being able to put your foot down on what's yours!" he shouts. He then walks over to Lamar slowly with a walk filled with confidence. "Look at you. All of your so-called skills are worthless. You'll never know what it's like to experience it. Hell even with your so called skills and technique you still managed to get rendered by a hotel worker and an old man who can barely drive, but don't worry I'll put you out of your misery very soon. That way you won't have to take any orders from me when I take over!" Valentine says. Lamar then chuckles. "What's so funny?" Valentine asks. Lamar smirks and says, "I see why they call you Valentine. You're too emotionally charged." Valentine then frowns and walks over to Lamar at a brisk pace. He places the large nail on Lamar's left pectoral muscle. "Hmm let's see if you'll be laughing after this!" Valentine shouts. Lamar knows that he has to react quickly; it's now or never. "This is how I got the name Valentine!" Valentine says. He takes the large hammer and reaches back to swing forward, but with all his brute force he's too slow to strike before Lamar counters by swiftly taking his free hand from behind his back and grabbing Valentine with a vicious grip to the throat region causing him to drop the hammer all while stopping him in his tracks somewhat, but it only slows Valentines attempted assault down as he still has the large nail pressed against Lamar's chest. Valentine continues to exert his strength forward attempting impale the rusty nail through Lamar's heart. Lamar takes his feet and kicks them up into Valentine's abdomen and pushes him back, but it still barley slows him down. Valentine continues his attempt to end him, but there's no quit in Lamar. He continues to push with all his strength even though he knows he's heavily out matched in strength. As the two continue to struggle with one another, suddenly the sound of flesh being impaled cracks through. Valentines facial expression changes from a straining frown into a look of shock. His eyes widen up in fear. His grip weakens from around the rusty nail. He steps back as Lamar falls to the floor backwards in the chair and rolls onto his feet. Valentine still in shock reaches his hand to the back of his head and neck region and turns around. Lamar notices the handle of a knife sticking out the back of Valentine's neck. Valentine wraps his right hand around the knife handle while reaching in front of him with his left hand in disbelief from what has just happened. He's angered by what has just occurred. "You traitor bitch!" He yells out in agony toward Alina. He hollers out and lunges forward, but Lamar quickly darts forward and enforces the knife even deeper into the back of Valentine's neck. Valentine falls back with all his weight atop Lamar in an attempt to shake him off his back, but Lamar continues to hold on. There's a slight struggle, but it's too late for Valentine. Lamar tightens his grip on the knife handle. Valentine's eyes gaze back as he slowly stops moving and breathes out his last breath. "Ahh" is the last sound that comes from his mouth. Lamar then feels all of Valentine's weight beginning to increase as his body becomes motionless. He then pushes Valentine's body to the side and slides from underneath the corpse. Lamar stands to his feet. He stares into Alina's eyes. With his bruised leg he limps over to her. He reaches out toward her and extends himself to give her a hug. As she opens her arms to accept him, suddenly he grabs her and throws her against the wall near the table of weapons used for torture and holds her up by her throat. He then grabs one of the knives from the table and puts the blade up to her throat. She's in fear for her life. "Are you still behind any of this?" He asks. She stares him in the eyes sternly and swallows air. "If I were behind any of this madness then I would've executed you back at the hotel after the job we did on The East River." She explains. Lamar strengthens his grip, "But you were intimate with him weren't you?" He yells out. "Yes. It may be hard for you to believe, but he was my husband." She says while grunting. "Why the sudden change of heart?" He asks. She grunts and then says, "Let me down and I'll tell you!" Lamar thinks about it. He soon releases his grip and she drops back to her feet.

"THE TRUTH"

Alina drops back down to her feet. She sighs in relief to still be alive. Lamar steps back with the knife still in his hand. "Talk" He says. She stares him in the eyes boldly. "The truth, the truth is that I was supposed to take out both you and the target, for the East River job, but I couldn't." She explains. "Why didn't you?" he asks. "Because I was also told not to; the truth is my loyalty is to Kristian and The Regime not the six factions. I was working as a double to cover my tracks. It was supposed to look like I was not with The Regime." She says. "Well that's obvious" Lamar says. "Kristian got himself into some hot water, so he figured with you he would bail himself out." She explains. "Why me?" Lamar asks in a surprising manner. "Because he knew you would be able to find a way to get through. He knew you weren't just going to go through it all with your eyes closed." She says. "What do you mean by that?" he asks. "Kristian knows what you are doing during the times you are alone. He knows that you fully think things through before you act on any of the orders he gives you." She explains. Lamar begins to speak then suddenly he hears a noise, soft footsteps striking the pavement outside the cellar. He runs over and pushes Alina to the side.

Behind Alina in the entrance of the cell stands a gunman armed to kill. Lamar dives in the same direction that he pushed Alina. The gunman fires off several rounds. He makes his way into the cell, but he is met with a flying dagger to his neck. Lamar rises to his feet quickly as he hears another set footsteps outside the door. He sprints with a limp and grabs the steel door and swings it just as the second gunman arrives. "Smack", the door hits the gunman as he tries to rush in. The impact dazes him as he is knocked backwards from the force of the steel door hitting him. Lamar quickly opens the door as the gunman tries to charge back into the cell. He grabs the gunman, puts him in a side headlock and snaps his neck. The gunman's body falls to the floor. Lamar looks down at him and he notices it's the same guy from the hotel who had tased him. "There's more on the way." Alina says. Lamar looks over at the surveillance camera in the corner. He picks up one of the gunmen's semi-automatic weapons takes aim at the camera and takes it out. Back in the surveillance room the guards inside frantically tell one another to get down to cell. Back inside the cell, Lamar says, "If there's more on the way then we don't have much time left." Alina briskly walks over and picks up the other gunman's weapon and says "Follow me; I know how to get out of here." "How do I know that I can trust you?" Lamar asks. "At this point you don't have any other choice." She responds. She quickly makes her way out the cell with Lamar following behind, but before he exits he snatches some of the blades from the table of torture. Alina stares at him in a surprising manner. He smiles and says, "May not have enough bullets." "Point taken." She says. They both proceed down the moist hallway. Lamar's leg seems to be causing him a great deal of pain, but he ignores it and keeps going. As they reach the end of the hall, Alina goes over to the corner on the right side and peaks around. She immediately spots enforcers outside the hallway waiting for her and Lamar. They begin to fire off rounds, but they only hit and chip away at the concrete walls and pavement. Alina braces herself and holds her weapon close. "How many" Lamar asks. "About eight; two on the stairs, two on the top balcony and four on the ground level." She responds. "Is there another way out?" Lamar asks. "Only one way in and one way out and that's through that surveillance booth at the top of the balcony. From there we'll have to take the elevator to get above ground." She explains. "Any ideas?" Lamar asks. She smiles and says "Not really." Lamar then tells her to stand back. He peaks around to take a quick look at the scene himself. The guards once again begin to fire off rounds, but Lamar manages to get a quick glance of the scenery. "Okay, I think I know what to do, but I won't be able to move as quick with this bum leg." He says. Alina steps in front of him and crotches down. "What are you doing?' He asks her. "Stand still, this will hurt a little." She says. She then pushes him back against the wall by his waist and rubs her hands down his right quad muscle. "Is the pain here?" She asks. He looks down at her and answers "Yes". Then within a split of a second she swiftly chops his bruised thigh. Lamar snaps his head back against the wall and grits his teeth in agonizing pain. He then stomps his right leg attempting to erase the pain. She stands against the wall next to him. "Better?" She asks. "I'll get there." He responds. She laughs then suddenly she pushes him out into the action. Lamar with his ability to react fast to what has just happened, rolls forward to his feet with the semi-automatic weapon aimed at one of the guards on the top balcony. He takes him out with one shot. He quickly takes aim at the other guard and does the same. He dodges the many bullets that are fired at him, but he knows he can't continue for long. Alina hangs from around the corner of the moist hallway and provides cover fire. She sprays many rounds at the four guards on the ground level. She manages to take out two of them before the other two run for cover. As they do so, Lamar aims upward again and attempts to fire at the guards on the stairs. Tick tick tick, his gun is jammed. As the two guards on the stairs continue to fire at him along with the two remaining guards on the ground level directly in front of him; He quickly pulls out two of the daggers he took from the table of torture in the cell. He knows the two guards on the stairwell are too high up for him to get an accurate strike on them, so he sprints forward toward the stairwell where the two guards on the ground level are located. Alina sees this and she quickly adjusts her focus to the two guards on the stairwell. She aims and pulls the trigger. One of the guards catches one right between the eyes and he falls down the stairs while the other is struck in the chest region and stomach and falls forward over the stair railing. The guard's body makes a loud slamming noise from the impact of the fall to the concrete floor. Meanwhile Lamar with blades in hand takes on the guards on the ground level. They fire but they are unable to hit him with any of their rounds. He swiftly moves through the traffic of projectiles coming his way effortlessly with an array of acrobatic skills and spins. He makes it to the first guard positioned between him and the second guard behind. The guard is disabled quickly with a slash to his neck region. Blood squirts out as he drops his weapon in an attempt to stop the blood from gushing out. Lamar grabs him, spins him around and uses him as a human shield against the other guard's firepower. "Give it up!" Lamar shouts out to the remaining guard, but the guard continues to fire off many rounds. The rounds pierce through the body of the guard Lamar is using as a shield. Lamar picks up the dead guard's weapon and aims it at the guard who is still shooting frantically. Lamar kicks the dead guard's body forward and dives to his left while still aiming at the frantic guard. He pulls the trigger. Two rounds ring out and nail the guard in the torso. As this happens Lamar notices another round from behind him hits the guard right in his face. Lamar looks back and notices Alina has come from around the corner. The guard drops to his knees with his mouth wide open in shock. He finally expires and falls flat on his stomach. Lamar gets to his feet and looks around to see if there's anyone else remaining, but the scene is quiet. Alina walks over toward him. "Next time warn me before you throw me to the wolves again!" Lamar says to her. She smiles "How else was I supposed to see what you're capable of." She replies. Lamar cracks a smile. "Let's get out of her." Alina says.

An elevator makes its way to the top of a shaft in a location that isn't known yet deep within a forest like environment, hidden off from the rest of civilization. The elevator comes to a stop at the top of the shaft. The doors open. Out steps Lamar and Alina. Lamar takes a look at the bunker like scene. "What is this place?" he asks. It's one of many personal prisons owned by the Factions." She explains. "Where are we?" Lamar asks. "North of Quebec, they transported you here from Monaco." She answers. "That explains everything." He responds. Alina turns to Lamar and stares at him. He stares back for a moment. "I have to get back to the compound to get the answers I need from Kristian." He says. "Follow me," she says. They walk over to one of the many military like vehicles and they proceed to enter one of the hummers. "I'll drive." She says.

"THE DRIVE"

Lamar's vision is filled with nothing but an empty paved snowy road, split between thousands of trees. The road seems to run on forever, but he knows eventually it will end. Until then he thinks to himself. "Now would be a good time to finish hearing some of the truth." "So what's your story? How did you become involved in this mess?" He asks. Alina takes her focus off the road for a split second and begins to speak. "About fifteen years ago I was in an orphanage with no mother or a father to come and get me. Just my older sister Angela and I. Our parents met near the end of the Cold War. My father was Palestinian and my mother was of Israeli descent. He met her during an attack in her native village. She saved him from some falling debris from one of the collapsing structures that were bombed by one of the military planes. Around the time I was twelve and Angela was fifteen; my parents were supposedly killed in a train that derailed off a bridge. My sister and I were then sent to live with one of my father's friends. Juan Manuel in Honduras, our time there was pleasant at first, but within months everything had changed. He was heavily involved with the armed forces there. Right around that time they were trying to crackdown on the cartel, but once they found out where Juan was living, it took a turn for the worse. It was late at night when they stormed in. They were armed with RPG's and various assault rifles. All I remember hearing was a blast, and then high-powered gunfire. I can remember hearing their voices speaking their native language. Angela tried her best to protect me. She had me lie flat on the floor while she pulled a mattress off the bed and placed it over me. I still remember her last words. 'Whatever happens, make sure you stay here until it's safe' She said. I can still remember the tears running rapidly down my cheeks. It was the last time I had seen her. When it was over; I finally came out to see what had occurred. Juan had been killed. He was executed along with his wife. I tried frantically to search for Angela, but she was nowhere to be found. I had lost everything. I couldn't even find her body throughout the wreckage. From there finally the military officers had arrived too late. All I could do was sit in front of what was once our home for the moment. I felt lost. Soon after I didn't receive much help from the authorities, they just put me in a van and sent me on about my way. From there I went to numerous places and I finally ended up in this orphanage in Bosnia. Being there was cruel and cold. I remember many nights without eating and sleeping on the cold hard floors. It all changed one day. One of the maids there told me someone was there to pick me up. That's when I met Kristian." She explains. Lamar cuts his eyes in a surprised reaction. He had experienced the same encounter with Kristian at a place strangely similar. "So that's how you became involved with the Regime?" He asks. "Yes, I've been with them ever since." She replies. He turns and stares at her and thinks to himself.

'Wow, she sure has one hell of a story.' "So what exactly is the Six Factions?" he asks. "It's a group made up of six different leaders who belong to an organization of their own. Together they make most of the important decisions that help determine the fate of everything that happens in the world. It used to be seven of them until the seventh leader died about thirty years ago. Ever since then they only operate as a six man family." She explains. "So they're the ones who control everything behind close doors?" Lamar asks. "Yes, and they don't tolerate anyone interfering in their decisions. That's were The Regime comes into play. They give the orders to our leader, who then passes them off to Kristian." Alina explains. "Our leader; I thought Kristian ran The Regime." Lamar says. "No he's just another part of the puzzle. He's only second in command." She says. "So have you ever met the head of The Regime?" Lamar asks. "No the only person who has been in contact with him is Kristian." She answers. Lamar then thinks to himself "I wonder who it may be?" "So what's the story between you and Valentine?" He asks. Alina then smirks and breathes out "Valentine, what is it you would like to know?" She asks. "Well how did you two become an item, and why did he turn?" Lamar asks. "Well I met him a few years after I had been bought in. he had been with The Regime for a long time. He was one of the best. He always finished his missions in the most convincing fashions. He was pretty much a perfectionist with his work. He made sure he went through every detail. He always made sure he left his signature after every execution. A long nail hammered into his targets chest. That's how he got his name. His real name was Victor Davis.

He specialized in torture as you may have noticed, but he was romantic when we first met. It was just his greed and jealousy of Kristian that drove us apart." She explains. "Why was he so jealous of Kristian?" Lamar asks. "Because Kristian is next in line to gain power if something were to happen to the head of The Regime. Valentine really began to despise Kristian to a high degree. They use to be close, but as time went on he really began to distance himself from Kristian, because he couldn't stand taking orders from someone who he felt like wasn't as good at getting the job done as well as him. Everything became a competition to him." She says. "So how did he end up with you?" Lamar asks. Alina turns and looks Lamar in the face. "Well like I said before, he was very romantic. We first encountered each other in a training session. He would always figure out a way to compliment me in a very strange, but sweet way." She says. Lamar turns his attention to the road in a nonchalant fashion as if he doesn't want to hear the rest, but he continues to listen. "Soon after that we had become close. He was very thoughtful of me at the time, but I noticed the change after Kristian got promoted to be second in command under the current head of The Regime. Valentine would become consumed by trying to prove he was better than everyone else. From there on he would become more brutal with his work. He would go overboard with what was asked of him. One day he had been contacted by one of the leaders of the Factions. He had been given an opportunity to join them, but under one circumstance. He was asked to spy on The Regime. As jealous and angry as he was, he agreed to it without hesitating. He came to me about it and told me everything. I couldn't believe it. He asked me to join him, but I didn't feel right about it. He was asking me to betray the same man who had saved me from a life of torment. I agreed with him to do it, but I immediately told Kristian in private. He was shocked by the news. He didn't want to believe it at first, but he became convinced after hearing one of Valentine's rants filled with jealousy and rage. Kristian was hurt by it. He had just learned that the person he thought was his closest confidant had been so envious of him for no apparent reason. I told him that they wanted me to be apart of their operation as well, but my allegiance is with him and The Regime. So he had me spy on them in return. I was at a crossroad. On this hand I had the man who I was in love with asking me to be apart of his come up under the radar, and on the other my loyalty to The Regime was being tested. I didn't know what to do, but it all changed once I was asked to spy on you." She explains. Lamar doesn't let her know that he already figured she was, instead he just keeps his cool and keeps his surprise in store for her hidden. "How long?" he asks. "Since your job in Vegas." She answers. He's surprised by her response. He then asks her "So the job in Shanghai wasn't the first?" She's shocked by his question. "What do you mean?" She asks with a slight smirk on her face. "On the bridge; I couldn't tell it was you at first, due to the monk like robe you were wearing." He says as he reaches over, grabs her wrist and rolls her sleeve back. "But you should've made sure you were fully covered." He explains. She stares at him while still smirking. "Interesting." She says. "What?" He asks. "It's interesting how you examine everything around you." She explains. "Well that's what the Regime taught us isn't it?" He asks. She smiles at his question. "I guess it's safe to assume that it was you who visited my room late at night." He says. She doesn't respond to his comment. There's much she has to say, but she's afraid to reveal the whole truth to him. Lamar knows there's more to the story and he's not going to stop until he knows the all the details of their current situation. "Well if you knew it was me, why didn't you say anything sooner?" She asks. He smirks and says, "I had to be sure, before I made a judgment." She remains silent. "So what happened back at the hotel after the East River job? Was that real or was it just part of your job? You know spying on me?" He asks. She then grips the steering wheel tightly with both hands and inhales deeply. She then exhales heavily, while closing her eyes for a brief second. She then opens them and finally gives in. "It was real." She says. "I never planned on it happening, it just did." She explains. Lamar looks over at her and then says "Hmm, that explains why the chamber of your gun was empty." She smiles and then says, "Kristian thinks very highly of you." "If he thinks so highly of me, why did he send me on vacation to die. It was practically a suicide mission." Lamar says somewhat in an angry manner. "He didn't like the thought of it, but one thing about Kristian is that he makes sure he thinks everything through before he makes a decision. Hence the hotel room being directly next to the pool and you were only seven floors up." She explains. "Kristian would send me to spy on you because he needed confirmation to see if you completed the task the way it's supposed to be performed." She explains. Lamar is fulfilled with her answer. He then turns his attention toward the road ahead. He notices that they are starting to approach civilization. As they pass by a gas station and resting stop. Alina notices an old lodging hotel of the wooded community. "We have to make a stop so we can get you cleaned up and switch cars." She says. "That sounds like a good idea. My leg is killing me." He responds. She chuckles at his statement. "What?" He asks. "Nothing, it's been a while since I've heard anybody admit that they were in pain. That's just something The Regime teaches us not to reveal. It's good to see there's still some humility left in some of us." She says. He is shocked by her explanation and laughs at the thought of it. The hummer comes to a stop. Alina puts the vehicle in park. "I'll get us a room, be back in a sec." She says. He nods his head in a yes motion. Alina smiles and then walks off to the office of the hotel lodge. Lamar sits back and looks around. He notices a heavyset man getting into his big rig. "Some life." He says to himself. He then turns his attention to an old lady walking over to her car. "Some life they must live." He thinks to himself. He stares at his battered leg and places his hand on it in an attempt to massage the pain. He grits his teeth in agony. He reclines back and recalls the events that have just taken place, specifically a flashback of Valentine attempting to impale a rusty nail through his chest. He recalls the moment that changed everything. When Alina impaled Valentine in the back of his neck with the knife. He recalls Valentine's last words. "You traitor!" He said. Lamar then asks himself. "If she betrayed him, will she betray me?" He pauses and thinks about it for a few. He then says to himself. "She's had many opportunities to do so at this point." He looks through the window of the lobby and stares at Alina while she speaks with the greeter of the lodge. Suddenly that feeling of intimacy kicks in. His heart begins to feels soft again. He inhales slowly and breathes out. Alina then stares back at him and rubs her hair from in front of her eye. She smiles and winks. He smirks back at her. He focuses back on his swollen quad muscle and begins to massage it to ease the pain somewhat. Suddenly he hears taps coming from the outside of the window of the vehicle. He raises his head up and sees that it's Alina on the other side of the window smiling with keys hanging from her fingers. He opens the door and steps out. "Does it come with room service?" he asks jokingly. "No but it does come with soup and stitches." She says as she helps him get out.

The sound of rapid drops of water hitting a tub made of clay opens the scenery of the bathroom in the hotel room filled with steam. Behind the shower curtain stands Lamar with his head under the water. He lets the water run off his head peacefully as he breathes out some stress.

Moments later he turns off the water, steps out and grabs a towel off the shelf next to the sink, and dries himself free of the water drops. He wipes the smoke from the mirror and stares in. He examines the bruises left on his face from the lead pipe Valentine struck him with. He takes his hand and rubs it against the bruise. The pain is still there, but not as present as it was at first. He looks down into the sink and gathers himself. He lifts his head up, closes his eyes and sighs. He walks over to the door and exits. As he opens the door he sees Alina sitting on the bed anticipating him to come out. "Hot enough?" she asks. He smiles and walks over to the bed and sits next to her. He grits his teeth as he plants himself down. She stares at him with a smile on her face. "Comfortable?" She asks. "Barely." He responds. Alina turns around and opens a case that she has placed next to her. "Well it gets worse before it gets better." She says. Inside the case there's a sharp blade along with needle and thread. She opens a bottle of alcohol and dips the blade in. "Remove your towel, this will only hurt for a second." She says. He removes the towel in an uncomfortable manner. She chuckles and says, "You act like this is the first time you've been bare around me!" He laughs in return. She takes the blade and slowly impales it into his swollen quad muscle. The pain is excruciating, but he remains calm and holds it all in. He looks down at his leg and watches as the blood and puss leak out. "Wow, it's a miracle you're able to still walk." She says as she cleans up the mess with a towel. She then grabs the needle and black thread. She dips the needle into the alcohol the same as she did with the blade. He watches her as she performs. "Who taught you how to stitch?" He asks. Alina in surprise catches herself and puts her head down and thinks. "Angela. My mother taught her when we were little. There was one time when her and I were playing around and I happened to have fallen and get a huge gash on my calf muscle. We were out where we weren't supposed to be. When we got back home, the bleeding had gotten worse. So she sewed it up. We hid it from Juan, because we didn't want him to know we had left the yard. It took about six weeks or so before I healed up." She explains. Lamar smirks. "Hmm it's good that you have many memories with your sister. Only memory I have of my family is my parents shooting poison into their veins." He tells her. "So what was your life like before The Regime?" She asks as she begins to stitch up his wounded leg. "Not fun." He answers. "My days back at the group home were not the best. At the time I felt like I was going to be stuck there forever." He explains to her. "Sounds all too familiar" she adds. "But the good thing that came from it was I learned how to protect myself from others. There were many times were I would get hounded and lynched by the kids who were much bigger than me. It was like the more and more they attacked me with every strike, I learned how to take it until I was able to fight back. Eventually I was able to take them all out one by one. The last one was the most brutal though…." Lamar explains.

"DIGGING IN THE PAST"

Detroit's Westside, home to the Stephenson group home for boys; a young face Lamar is taking his dish of torment from a heavyset black kid who is more than twice his size. The heavyset black kid pushes Lamar around. He slaps him a few times in the face. "You aren't going to do anything." The heavyset kid yells at Lamar. His words make Lamar tick and he finally reaches a boiling point. Lamar charges at the heavyset kid and delivers a bald toe kick to his shin, causing the heavyset kid to yell in agony. The heavyset kid charges forward in anger. Lamar steps to the side quickly and sticks his foot out tripping the kid, causing him to fall face first into the brick wall. The heavyset kid is disoriented, but Lamar doesn't show any mercy. He begins kicking and stomping down on the fat kid's ribs cracking two of them. Lamar is breathing heavily. Suddenly from behind the shadows dressed in a custodial outfit is a younger version of Kristian. He's impressed by Lamar's work. "I've found my perfect candidate." He says with a smile on his face. Lamar stops and stares at Kristian. He then asks, "What do you mean?" Kristian sighs and says "A representative or a front man. What's your name kid?" Lamar stares at Kristian with a strong sense of nervousness. "What's it to you?" Lamar asks. "Well my name is Kristian, I'm from Germany. That's all I can tell you for now kid." Kristian then exhales out. "So are you going to tell me your name kid?" He asks. Lamar now with a sense of calmness from Kristian then speaks. "Lamar" He answers. "Ahh Lamar, such a name, how did you get it?" Kritistian asks. "My father, he had the same name as I." Lamar responds. "Hmm what happened to him?" Krisitian asks. "Long story and I don't have time to tell it all." Lamar says. "Well I hope to find out." Kristian responds. "Yeah whatever" Lamar says as he begins to exit the basement. As he walks past, Kristian stares at him with a sinister smile on his face.

"WAKING DISCOVERY"

It's early the next morning. One of the supervisors is making her way down to the basement to get some supplies, only to discover the heavyset kid that Lamar has put a hurting on laying on the floor in agony. She then checks on him by putting her hand on his shoulder. The kid screams out so loud that his pain echo throughout the basement. The supervisor then asks him "What happened?" "Lamar, Lamar did this to me!" The kid says.

"POLICE SIRENS CRY"

I t's a cold chilly morning as the police enter Lamar's room. He is sitting on the top bunk of an old bunk bed. As they enter he doesn't move. He just sits and stares out the window at the blue and grey morning tone filled with snow on the pavement. The officers scream out to Lamar "Step down and lay flat on the floor!" He hears them, but he is so deep in thought he pays it no mind. They yell out again. "Step down and lay flat on the floor!" He ignores them once again. The officers then rush and pull Lamar from the bunk and slams him face first to the floor. They then cuff him. As they restrain him, he spits blood out his mouth caused from a cut created on the inside of his lip from the officers restraining him. They then lift him up to his feet. As they escort Lamar from the building. He breathes out a sigh of relief as the cold wind blows against his face. They then throw him in the back seat of their cruiser. As the car pulls off, Lamar feels relieved that he no longer has to put up with the ills of the group home any longer. Though he does not know what will happen next, he is glad to finally make his exit.

Kristian is just now arriving to the scene of Lamar being escorted to the police cruiser. He's dressed in his custodial gear. The police cruiser pulls off with Lamar secured inside. Kristian smiles and says, "It's time." He speeds down the street after the cruiser. He reaches to his right and opens up the middle console of his Buick and pulls out a nine millimeter with a silencer suppressed to it. As the police cruiser comes to a red light, Kristian pulls along side them. He lowers down his passenger side window as if he needs to ask the officers something. The one officer who is driving then lowers down his window as well. Kristian yells out. "Can you tell me how to get to Interstate 75?" The officer proceeds to answer as he points his finger out the window. Kristian sees the perfect opportunity while everything is occurring. Lamar sits in the back seat with his head down staring at his feet. He recognizes Kristian's voice. As he raises his head; Kristian with his sinister grin on his face without hesitating lifts up the gun and pulls the trigger. The officer behind the wheel gets hit between the eyes. Blood spatters out. His lifeless body leans forward onto the steering wheel. His partner reaches for his side arm in fear, but he's too late. Kristian releases a second shot. The bullet travels and hits the panicky officer in the temple. He's knocked to the right and hits the window from the force of the shot. Lamar looks on with a sense of confusion. Kristian then exits his vehicle and begins walking over toward the police cruiser. He leans down and stares at Lamar. "Time to go kid" He says. "You're not going to kill me?" Lamar asks. "Kill you? No Kid, you're too much of a talent to be wasted!"

"Back to the Present"

"I just remember having that feeling of being free from it all once it was over. At first I just thought Kristian was some German immigrant working another dead end job, but it was obviously a front." Lamar explains. Alina is almost done with the stitches. As she finishes up she jokingly says. "I guess we both turned out to be model citizens." Lamar laughs in response to her remark. "Yeah we're both screwed up individuals." He says. Alina laughs as she cuts and ties the thread off. As their laughter fades, they stare into one another's eyes and become silent. Alina bats her eyes and kisses him on the cheek. She pulls back in a shy manner. Lamar then grabs her by the back of her head, pulls her in close and they begin to lock lips slowly. The mood between them becomes intense. As Lamar rips open her black shirt and softly caresses his hands on her breast. They continue to kiss passionately. Alina then becomes aggressive, by pushing him back and climbing on top of him. She begins to kiss and lick his neck eventually moving down to his chest region. He grabs a handful of her hair and pulls her back to his face and they begin to aggressively kiss one another again. Lamar begins to unbutton her black pants and unzips them. He pulls them off her revealing her underwear. They turn over as the roles become reversed. He then grabs the handles of her panties and slowly pulls them off her. He then grabs her legs and pulls her close. He positions himself between her legs. As he begins to insert himself inside her, he leans in and kisses her intensely. She begins to moan. She kisses him even more aggressively as she bites his bottom lip causing him to bleed somewhat. They continue to show one another affection. Lamar turns her over with her back facing him. He continues as she lies on her stomach while she stretches her head back to continue kissing him. He grips her hands tightly as the intimacy heats up between them. They both climax almost simultaneously. She turns around, stares at him and smiles. Lamar leans in and they begin to softly kiss one another.

They both lie in one another's arms and enjoy each other's company. They begin to pillow talk about themselves to one another with little time they have left before they make their way back to the compound. "What's your favorite weapon of choice?" Lamar asks her. She smiles "I would have to say a rifle of any kind. No matter what it is, I know how to shoot it." She says. "I'm not surprised!" Lamar responds. "What do mean?" She asks. "Well judging by the job on the East River, I pretty much figured you was fond of rifles." He says. "So what's your favorite?" She asks. "I wouldn't know. I just do what I have to in order to get the job done." He responds. "Come on, you have to choose one!" She says. "Like I said, I don't have one, but I do prefer something that's quick and painless. Whenever I use a blade, whoever the target is last emotion or reaction sticks with me." He explains. "I've never really experienced that before. The usual reaction I get from them is either they just collapse without knowing what just happen or they open their mouths wide and fall out flat." She explains. "Have you ever wondered what the people you've terminated were like, who they were or what they did that was so wrong to have their life taken?" He asks. "No, I've never really took out the time to think about that. I usually just do and don't ask." She answers. He chuckles at her response. "What?" She asks. "Nothing, it's just that you sound like you were reading an instruction manual given to you by The Regime." He responds. "Well that's what they've instilled in us right?" She asks. "Yes, it is." He says. "Have you ever thought about your future or where you're headed?" She asks. "Not really, well there's been a few times late at night when I stare out my window and wonder what life would be like had my up bringing been filled with happiness and family, but I've never given much thought about the future." He explains. "Hmm, I guess that's what a life of taking orders will do for you." She says. Lamar thinks about her statement and realizes that she's right. "I guess we live a life of continued cycles." He says. "What do you mean by that?" She asks. "Being part of The Regime is not too much different from the past conditions of our lives. You either take orders, follow directions or you get punished. It's all the same. I'm thankful that The Regime has saved me from a life of physical torment, but I still deal with the mental torment. The nightmares, the faces of the targets I've eliminated and their last reactions. Back when I was living in the group home I had some sense of free will and thinking. With The Regime,

I have to hide it all and not reveal myself." He explains. "I've never thought of that way, but in some sense you're right." She responds. She then takes Lamar's hand and begins to massage it. "So how do you feel now?" She asks. Lamar thinks for a second. "How do I know I can trust you?" He asks. "What exactly do you mean?" She asks. "How do I know if you won't do me like you did Valentine?" He asks. "If I wanted you dead, I would've let him impale that long nail through your chest. I would've just taken you out during the job on the East River, or I could've let you freeze to death." She answers. He cracks a smile at her answer. "Hmm how do I feel right now?" He asks out loud. "Come on, you can tell me, your secret's safe with me." She says. He finally gives in. "I feel like I finally understand the experienced of being loved. It's like a huge weight has been lifted off my shoulders, just for a little while." He explains. She looks at him and smiles. "I too feel the same way." She says.

"A HEARTFELT NIGHTMARE"

The scenery is smoky and filled with fog. Lamar finds himself tied down to a chair. As he looks around he notices a massive grisly silhouette figure standing in front of him. He wonders who it is. Then suddenly the person begins to step forward becoming more visible for him to see. Lamar notices the grisly figure has a hammer and long nail in hand. The figure continues to slowly reveal itself with each step it takes into the light. Suddenly a voice begins to speak as the figure gets up close to Lamar. "Now you'll see why they call me Valentine!" The voice says. Lamar feels defenseless as he sits and waits for what's next. Then suddenly there's a flash of Valentine's face as he takes his massive hammer with nail and begins to impale Lamar in the chest. Within an instant Lamar comes to a wake. He breathes out frantically. He then takes his hands and rubs them over his face filled with sweat. His movements and sounds awaken Alina. She sits up and stares at him for a second. She then takes her right hand and begins to massage his back. "Another nightmare?" She asks. He shakes his head and motions yes. He calms himself down. "What was it about?" She asks. He turns toward her and shakes his head in a no like motion. "Come on tell me. What was it?" She asks. He still refuses to tell her. "Nothing just an old face." He tells her. "Who?" She asks. He reluctantly answers "Valentine". "Hmm" She says. "What is it?" He asks. "I just don't understand what happened between he and I." She explains. Lamar doesn't say anything at first. He's still trying to recover from his nightmare. "Maybe you were just looking to see what it was like to be loved." He says to her. "I guess." She responds with a look of wonder in her eyes. "Get some more sleep. We don't have too much time left before we have to leave out." She says. They hug and cuddle with one another and proceed to go back to sleep.

"SUNRISE"

Lamar wakes at the sound of an alarm next to the bed. He hears water drops of sprinkling water hitting the inside of the clay bathtub in the bathroom. He rises out the bed. As he stands to his feet, Alina steps foot from the bathroom dressed in a white robe. "How's the leg?" She asks. He turns his attention to his leg and examines it. "Much better" he says as he stomps his foot on the floor. She smiles "I told you I knew what I was doing." She says. He cracks a smile in return. "I suppose." He responds.

The sound of airplane jet engines sets off the scenery of the Airport in Quebec. Lamar and Alina make their way through the pedestrian traffic. She turns to Lamar and says "Alright we have to separate for the time being." "How come?" He asks. "Because they're watching us right now as we speak" She explains. He wants to grab her and give her a goodbye kiss, but he knows what she has said is true, so they walk away from one another in separate directions. He looks back as she walks away. He turns around and continues to walk in the opposite direction. He still does not fully understand what's going on. "I have to get to the bottom of this." He says to himself.

"REVELATIONS EXPLAINED"

The scenery of the mountains and forest surrounding the compound are quiet and calm. The sound of the usual all black luxury car pulling up to the compound breaks through. The car comes to a stop. "Welcome home." The driver says. Lamar cuts his eyes to him but he remains silent. He steps out the car dressed in his fully black trench coat. He waits until the car pulls off like usual. Once the car does so, he walks over to the door and knocks. The door opens. On the other side Lamar notices one of the young prodigies opening the door. He examines the young one and thinks. "I wonder what dysfunctional background he came from?" As Lamar walks in, he notices there's plenty of movement throughout the place. It's almost as if they are preparing for war, or an attack of some sorts. "Welcome back!" The rusty voice of Kristian's German accent breaks through all the action. Lamar cuts his eyes to Kristian in a stern manner. He doesn't say a word. "Wait. I know what you are thinking. Come with me so I can explain it all to you!" Kristian says. Lamar reluctantly agrees and begins to walk with

Kristian as he begins talking and explaining everything.

"REVELATION WHILE WALKING"

Lamar and Kristian casually walk down one of the many hallways of the compound. As they walk both of them place their hands behind their back. "Well kid, I know I've got plenty of explaining to do. That wasn't a vacation that you were sent on. It was more of a test. Lamar turns to him and asks "A test?" "Yes I know kid. I have never trained you for that type of mission before, but I still have much faith in you. I knew you would have pulled through without a question." Kristian says in excitement. "Well that's one hell of a way to show someone that you believe in them." Lamar says. "Ha ha ha, you know kid, I never knew you had such a great sense of humor." Kristian says. Lamar remains silent and continues to listen. "Usually when I speak to you or give you advice, you just sit there and soak it all in. That's a trait that I once possessed when I first arrived here." Kristian explains. "Really, as much as you talk; I would have never thought that." Lamar says jokingly. "Yes kid, I was once like you when I first arrived here. I didn't speak or socialize with any one. I would always remain quiet, observe and analyze my environment. That way I wouldn't miss a single detail. I like to call it the mind of the carpenter. You know when The Regime first started up; it was formed by a group of carpenters, that way whenever it was time for completion of a mission, no detail would be left out." Kristian explains. "Yes I've been given somewhat of a history lesson already." Lamar responds. "So what was the deal between you and Valentine?" He asks Kristian. "Hmm, he and I walked the same path most of the time. We arrived here around the same time. I arrived a few months before him, but we became friends during that time period. We were almost like brothers. At the time it was unusual for a German and an African American to be friends, but we made it happen. I noticed the change in him once I became second in command. He became extremely obsessed with the thought of being a better assassin than I. He became more reckless with his style of execution. My mentor didn't like how he displayed himself. So he began demoting him. Once this happened, the angrier Valentine became. He started reaching out to the leaders of the Six Factions. He started telling them everything that goes on around this place." Kristian explains. "Six Factions" Lamar says as if he is surprised. "Yes kid the Six Factions. I'm pretty sure Alina has already filled you in on some of the details." Kristian says. He now knows that Kristian already knows most of his recent struggles and debacles for survival. "So I take it that she told you everything that has happened." Lamar replies. "Not everything, but yes she's already contacted me kid. We don't have too much time. Today is your lucky day kid; you get to meet the wisest of all men who have walked through these halls. He pretty much knows everything about the Six Factions. We are preparing for them now as we speak." Kristian explains. "Preparing for what?" Lamar asks. "Well as you may know by now; The Factions are preparing to eliminate us all. Due to the sweat off our backs they have now become powerful enough to get rid of us all and carry out their own orders of business. Somehow throughout the years they've managed to build and create their own groups of assassins, and they're all top tier. You and Alina are the only two from The Regime that come close to matching their skill levels." Kristian explains. "So are we going to war?" Lamar asks. "No, we're preparing for an attack. No matter what happens to me, we need to make sure you and Alina both survive. Especially you kid." Kristian replies. "Why do you need me to survive?" Lamar asks. "Because you have the magic eye to see everything, you are the complete soldier. You may not understand exactly what I'm saying right now, but in time you will." Kristian explains. Lamar turns toward Kristian and says, "That's a great deal of pressure to put on one's shoulders." "I know, but I'm sure you will be able to manage kid." Kristian says. They come to a stop at the end of the hall. Kristian then walks up to the wood grain wall and place his right palm against it. Lamar watches as the contents of the wall change shape and open up. The wall opens up to a passageway with stairs that lead down to a lower level. They both walk in. Lamar can smell the vapors in the air as they step down each step. They make their way to the bottom of the steps and turn a corner. As they come around from the dark corner, Kristian speaks out. "Well kid, here's the wise man that controls this entire organization." Lamar takes a look at him and sees it's a familiar face. "Him"

He says once the man is revealed. "He's just the driver." Lamar adds. "Yes that's what many believe." The so-called wise man says as he walks toward Lamar with his hand extended outward to shake Lamar's hand. "Yes I'm the wise one, or what you may believe to be nothing more than a chauffer." He says. Lamar then thinks, "Well it's the perfect cover to use as a disguise. Plus he's up there in age from the looks of things." "Welcome kid, my name is Verizio Borislav. I've been watching you for some time now. It amazes me how many times I've seen you leave this place and return in one piece. You are definitely a rare breed." The wise man says. Lamar is not moved by the old man's admiration. He just observes every word being spoken. "Well do you have any questions for me?" Verizio asks. "Not any that I could think of at the moment." Lamar replies. "Are you sure? Because from here on out you will be asked to act without question or hesitation in your every movement." Verizio explains. Lamar takes little time to think about it. "Well I do have one question in particular, how do you receive the orders to give out and carry on with"" He asks. "Well I receive them from each leader of the Factions. They contact me and send me all the data I need to pass on to my second in command Kristian." Verizio explains. Kristian stands behind Verizio quietly. Verizio then goes on to discuss more. "You know kid I've seen that you have a knack for asking the right questions when need be. That's a great quality to have." He says. The old man cracks a smile. Then from the shadows behind Verizio and Kristian, the silhouette figure of Alina begins to approach the light. She's dressed in her usual all black attire made of silk spandex and black jeans. She makes eye contact with

Lamar. She doesn't give off her usual smirk or smile towards him. Lamar remains silent and observant. "You see kid; everything is set in place thus far, now all we have to do now is wait." Kristian explains. "Wait for what?" Lamar asks. "Patience kid, the time will soon come." Kristian says. "Right now I need you to come with me. I have some very valuable information for you." Kristian adds. Lamar begins to walk with Kristian as he was asked. As they walk past Verizio, Lamar takes a good look at him. "Something is not right about this guy." He thinks to himself. Verizio smiles and winks as Lamar and Kristian walk past. Lamar then stares at Alina as he continues to walk with Kristian. She stares back at him and nods her head as if she's in agreement with Lamar's self contained thought. "Something definitely fishy here" Lamar thinks to himself.

"UNCOVERING THE SIX"

Lamar and Kristian make their way to a room in the back of the underground structure. Kristian then opens the door and they both walk in. After they walk inside, the room lights up. It's an all white scheme that separates it from the rest of the compound. "I know there's plenty thoughts going through your mind at the moment kid, but I assure you that I will look out for your best interest." Kristian explains. "What I have to tell you right now is very valuable information that you have to make sure you keep track of, in order to ensure that there is hope for you and the rest of the world's salvation from the controls of the Factions." Kristian says. Lamar is in a surprised state of mind. "Salvation" He asks. "Yes kid, I need for you to continue on, even if I don't make it. You are the one who will be able to continue our existence along with Alina. I know it sounds like it's too much, but I wouldn't place this responsibility upon your shoulders, if I didn't think you could not fulfill it." Kristian explains. Lamar then feels a funny feeling within the pit of his stomach. He hasn't felt this way since Kristian rescued him from the back of the police cruiser years earlier. "You can't ask that of me. How do you know if I'll be able to fulfill everything that you are asking of me?" Lamar says in reaction to all of Kristians demands. Kristian with a stern look in his eyes stares at Lamar "Because I've trained you to be the best. I've been preparing you for this day since we first met. Whether you want to believe it or not, but if you want to survive and gain your freedom, you're going to have to go through this process." Kristian responds. "Now suck it up, there's no time for getting scared or worried." Kristian shouts. Lamar turns toward him and says "I'm ready, what is it that you have for me?" he asks. "That's the spirit kid." Kristian replies. He walks over to a projection screen and presses a button to power it up. As the screen powers up, six photos appear upon the screen. "These are the faces of the Six Factions." Kristian says. Lamar takes a good look at all of them and examines their features. "These six men control all political decisions that go on in this world. They spread their power throughout the six continents where there is human population." Kristian explains in detail. Lamar notices that all the men in the pictures are quite elderly and they all seem to have the same posture as Verizio. Though he notices their characteristics, he doesn't say anything. Kristian then takes a remote and begins to go through all the pictures and profiles the men in the photos one by one. The first picture is a photo of a Japanese male. "Here we have the first of the six. Akiyo Chiyoko. He has power over most of East Asia. He used to share power with the seventh Faction leader until he perished thirty years ago. Now he is believed to be the sole controller of it all." Kristian explains. The projection then changes to a photo of a French man by the name of Mark Lawrence. "This fellow here controls all power within Europe. He's very high in class. Next we have another French man, but he's not European, he's African. Gustav Leonard. He's located in South Africa. Nobody really knows how he operates, but it's believed that he is responsible for eighty percent of the entire continent of Africa. Whatever he wants, he gets plain and simple. Next up we have two of your local countrymen. These two are right under the nose of the entire U.S. government and power. Here to your right we have Congressman Kevin Smith. To your left we have Congressman Vincent Jefferson. These two have been in power the longest out of all the six members of the Factions. They control everything in North America and many other locations. These two are extremely low- key. You wouldn't notice them if you see them crossing the street on a sunny day. Last but not least we have Leonardo Ricardo. He's very tricky. Almost anything involving narcotics and shipment within South America and Central America is controlled through him. He's truly a man of many riches." Kristian explains. Lamar examines all the info and then asks, "Do you have more detailed background info on them?" "Kid you always ask the right questions. I've made you a copy of all this info and more." Kristian answers as he reaches into his pocket and pulls out a USB travel drive. He tosses it over to Lamar who catches it and stares at it." Everything you need to know is on there. Makes sure you keep up with it. It is very critical that you not lose it because everything in this room will be destroyed." Kristian explains. "I will." Lamar replies. "Good, now let's get out of here and prepare for what's next." Kristian says as he walks over to open the door to exit the room. As he opens the door Lamar asks "What's next?" Suddenly standing on the other side of the door is Verizio with an evil frown upon his face stops Kristian in his tracks. "Yes boss, is there something wrong?" Kristian asks. "No everything is fine." Verizio answers. Then within an instant Verizio pulls out a pistol with a silencer and shoots. The bullet enters into Kristian's chest region. Kristian in a state of shock falls to the floor gripping his chest. Verizio then turns his attention to aiming the pistol at Lamar. "No need to finish him off. He's already been dying slow for the past thirty years now." Verizio says. Lamar is still in shock as to what has just taken place. "Is there anything you would like to add?" Verizio asks. Lamar doesn't respond. He just stands in silence and stares in anger at Verizio. "Snap out of it!" Verizio yells out. He then directs Lamar to come out the room, while still at gunpoint. Lamar slowly walks out. As he steps through the doorway and over an ailing Kristian, he notices behind Verizio, Alina is being restrained by a massive muscular male with a distinctive blade held at her neck region. "What's all this?" Lamar asks. "There seems to be a change in plans kid. This entire place is bound to be destroyed, but before I do so, I was wondering if you would like to join me and the Seven Factions?" Verizio asks. "Seven!" Lamar says in surprise. "I thought there were only six?" He says. "Ha, ha, ha, ha" Verizio laughs out hysterically. "Yes the very effects of a surprise are always entertaining, but seriously, I would hate to see such a great talent like you be wasted in such a tasteless manner. So what do you say?" Verizio asks. Lamar steps back "No" he answers. "Are you sure about your decision? If you join me I will give you everything you could possibly imagine and more!" Verizio responds. Lamar already has his mind made up. "No!" he says once again. "Very well, have it your way then. Vapex!" Verizio calls out to the muscular bound guy who is holding Alina captive. "Kill them quickly. Make sure no one leaves this palce alive." Verizio says. Lamar then abruptly asks, "So who are you supposed to be?" "I'm the one and only leader of the Seventh Faction." Verizo says. Lamar is not surprised by his answer. "So what was the whole point of you trying to control The Regime?" he asks Verizio. "I took over The Regime simply because all of you were getting out of control. I had to monitor you all to make sure you didn't have a sudden surge in power and right now it's time to shut it all down. Sorry to see such great prospects like your self go to waste. Good bye kid" Verizio says as he turns around and begins to walk away and make his exit from the basement like structure, but he leaves behind the humongous sized man who still has Alina within his restraints. "Take care of it!" Verizio demands as he exits up the stairs and closes the door behind him. Vapex doesn't say a word as he continues to hold Alina captive. Lamar stands and waits for the right moment to make his move without costing Alina her life. They stand at a still until Alina locks eyes with Lamar. She notices the travel drive in Lamar's hand. She motions her eyes upward. Lamar without hesitating tosses the small metal covered USB in the air all while simultaneously Alina takes her right foot dressed with black slim boots with heels attached and stomps down onto Vapex's foot impaling through his combat boot right into his foot. His grip weakens. Alina then drops free from his hold as Lamar runs into the attack. She dives forward and catches the USB as Lamar jumps through the air with a swift kick to Vapex's torso, but the impact from his kick only sends Vapex back a few steps. Vapex regains his ground and begins to laugh. "You two don't have a chance. You Regime rejects have been only trained to obey; you idiots are only called in to do light work. I've been sent to do many hellacious missions that have required way more than a few measly knives and guns!" Vapex says. Alina moves in closer to Lamar. "He's right. The assassins for the Factions have been well more advanced in their training compared to that of The Regime, but we still have a chance together." She says. Lamar then turns his focus to Vapex who has just pulled out two distinctive swords with sharp tips on the blades. "Prepare for you ending." He yells out. Vapex sprints toward Lamar and Alina quickly. Lamar pushes Alina to the side and attempts to counter Vapex's attack. Vapex moves in with a swift swing with both arms. Lamar extends his hands out and grabs hold both of Vapex's wrists restricting his attack temporarily, but Vapex delivers a kick to Lamar's abdominal region, weakening his defenses somewhat, but he manages to keep his grip on Vapex's wrist, shielding away from the attack. Vapex becomes more vicious with his attack, he increases his strength and lack of mercy and begins to take his knee and continues to strike Lamar's abdominal region numerous times until Lamar loosens his grip on his wrist's causing him to release Vapex's arms. Vapex then attempts to strike Lamar with his swords, but from behind Alina grabs him by his neck region in an attempt strangle him from behind. Vapex lets up on his attack on Lamar and focuses on Alina who has a tight hold on his neck. He reaches back and grabs her arms and leans forward, flipping her over his back onto the hard cemet ground. Alina falls on her back causing her to be temporarily dazed. Vapex then takes his swords and attempts to impale her as she lays at his feet, but Lamar jumps back into action with a full force punch to the back of Vapex's neck. He then follows up with a swift kick to Vapex's lower back sending him forward. Lamar notices a small blade falls from Vapex's waist. Alina grabs hold of it. Lamar without hesitating sprints at Vapex full speed and attempts to strike him with a combination. He lands the first punch to Vapex's face, with a second punch nailing him in the body, then a third to his ribs. Lamar's attack doesn't cause any damage. Vapex then grins with a sadistic smile and shakes his head at Lamar in shame. He then swings with his left arm and strikes Lamar with a back hand punch sending Lamar's body swinging to the left. Lamar is dazed by the attack. Vapex runs over to him and begins to stomp down into Lamar's stomach numerous times until he begins to cough up blood. "Hmm, I smell death!" Vapex says. He takes his sword and prepares to impale Lamar in his torso, but once again Alina comes in for the save; jumping onto Vapex's back, taking her finger nails and raking them into his eyes causing him to be temporarily blinded, but he takes his right arm and delivers an elbow into her ribs, causing her to gasp for air. He then takes his left hand reaches back grabbing her by a handful of hair and throws her forward. Alina is sent flying into the hard concrete wall knocking her head against it causing her to loose conscious. Lamar sees what happens to her and rises to his feet quickly. He runs over to aid her, but she's not responding. Meanwhile Vapex regains his sight and begins to laugh. "What do you know, only one bird left to kill now." He says. Lamar feels helpless, but he doesn't give up. Vapex sprints forward in full force with his swords aimed directly at Lamar's chest. Lamar barely dodges the attack by reacting and stepping aside causing the barbaric soldier to impale the cement wall. Lamar attempts to counter with a combination of attacks to the side of Vapex's ribs and face, but once again like the other attacks Lamar has attempted, Vapex shakes it off and grabs Lamar by the throat and slamming him against the wall. Lamar tries to fight off Vapex's hold, but he's too strong. He continues to hold Lamar against the wall as he grabs one of his swords that are stuck in the cement wall. "Time to end this!" Vapex says. He takes the sword and sticks it to Lamar's chest with the point of the blade against his chest. He begins to slowly impale him, but Lamar grabs the blade attempting to stop his execution. The sharpness of the sword slices into Lamar's hand causing his hand to bleed profusely and heavily, but the pain from the cuts won't stop his will to live. He continues to fight off the presence of death gripping the sword's edge tightly. Then suddenly the sound of a small blade slashing through Vapex's right leg breaks through. He looks down to discover that Alina has regained her conscious. Lamar sees an opening. He takes one of his hands off the blade's edge and hits Vapex with a swift chop to his throat, causing him to step back and grasp his throat to recover from the impact of Lamar's attack. Lamar becomes aggravated. He begins to feel how he felt when he lashed out at the heavy set kid back at the group home all those many years ago. He sprints toward Vapex with a fiery presence of focus in his eyes. He swiftly swings a punch to Vapex's throat region again, but Vapex blocks it by grabbing Lamar's right hand, but Lamar counters with a swift sweeping kick to Vapex's leg. The impact from the kick causes Vapex's knee to snap. Vapex then hunches over in pain. He tries to keep a straight face, but Lamar knows he's hurt. "Finally causing some damage, but it won't work." Vapex says. Vapex darts forward, but Lamar manages to spin around and maneuver behind him. He jumps onto Vapex's back and puts him in a chokehold with a tight grip. Lamar then wraps his legs around the back of Vapex's torso causing a more intense grip. Vapex tries to reach his hand behind him in an attempt to grab Lamar and throw him off, but every time he lunges forward he fails to get him off, due to Lamar having his legs wrapped tightly around his torso. Lamar holds and listens as Vapex's breaths began to decrease slowly. Vapex's wounded leg gives out casing him to fall on his side. Lamar doesn't let up on his grip. He continues to maintain his tight lock around Vapex's neck, constricting him of oxygen. "This can't be happening!" Vapex says in shock and fear. Lamar continues to restrict him of his air as Vapex attempts to strike Lamar in the ribs with his elbow. Lamar feels the impact of the heavy blows, but he doesn't fold, he continues to choke Vapex. "I can't die at the hands of a peasant!" Vapex shouts out while reaching both of his hands up into the air. He strikes Lamar with both his elbows this time connecting into Lamar's lungs. Lamar's grip weakens. Vapex then grabs hold of Lamar's arms and throws them away. He rises to his feet coughing and gasping for air. He then smiles. "I knew it. You won't ever be strong enough to take on the Factions." Vapex says as he begins laughing. Then suddenly from behind

Vapex, Alina sneaks in and impales his stomach. Vapex looks down at his gut in surprise. "What?" he says. Alina then removes the blade and quickly impales him in his lower back region. She leaves the blade in. Vapex falls to his knees with his eyes widen. Lamar gets to his feet as Alina stands behind Vapex breathing heavily. "You're nothing but a bunch of weak dogs, I can't believe this." Vapex struggles to get out his last words. Lamar then stares Vapex into his eyes with a fierce stare. Lamar with all his strength kicks Vapex in his throat sending him backwards onto his back. His body slams against the pavement causing the blade in his lower back to extend more throughout his body. He lays back while his eyes begin to glaze over and he breathes out his last breath. Lamar stares at the lifeless corpse of Vapex, and then suddenly a sound of someone moving comes from the corner. Lamar's eyes quickly switch over to the direction where the sound just came from. He notices it is Kristian he's still alive, but barely. Lamar and Alina both run over to aid him. Kristian turns over to lie on his back. Lamar takes a knee and grabs his hand. Kristian laughs out "Kid you've managed to prove your critics wrong again!" He says. Lamar smiles at Kristian's statement. "Look kid, I don't have much time to explain anything else to you." Kristian struggles to get out. He continues struggling to catch his breath. "Listen kid, I've set some things aside for you in a locker." He begins to explain as he reaches into his pocket and pulls out a small piece of paper. "Take this. On there you'll find the address. Everything you'll need will be in there." He says. Lamar takes the small piece of paper. "Take care kid, and remember, it's up to you to gain your salvation." Kristian says. "I know" Lamar replies.

"You know kid, you've been like the son I never had." Kristian explains. Lamar smiles at his comment. Kristian then closes his eyes and breathes out his last breath. Lamar is somewhat saddened, but he doesn't show it. Kristian's grip becomes lighter as Lamar holds his hand. Alina leans over and places her hand on Lamar's shoulder comforting his sadness somewhat. "We've to get going. Soon they'll be sending re-enforcements down here." She says. Lamar loosens his grip from Kristian's lifeless hand and stands to his feet. "Come on let's go." Alina says. They both gather themselves and make their way to the exit of the basement structure.

"A GRIM DISCOVERY"

The door opens into the hall of the ground level of the compound. Out steps Lamar and Alina. They both walk down the hallway only to discover plenty lifeless bodies of some of the young prodigies throughout the compound. They both look around amongst the grisly scene in shock. They begin moving forward through the grim scene. Suddenly there's a slight noise that echoes throughout the hall. Lamar cuts his eyes to the door on his left. He reaches over to the doorknob and turns it. He pulls the door open slowly. He looks in and notices that it is the young boy who greeted him earlier. The boy is crouched down hiding in a fetal position. He looks up with fear in his eyes. Lamar stares at the young one in amazement that he is still alive. Lamar extends his hand out to help the boy, but the young one still pulls back in fear. "Come on, I'm not going to hurt you." Lamar says in a sincere manner, but the young boy still does not accept Lamar's hand. Alina gives Lamar a slight shove to the side. "Hmm, let me give it a try." She says. Alina then extends her hand out to the young boy. The young one looks up into her eyes, suddenly his expression changes somewhat. The boy reaches his hand out in return, but he reluctantly reaches back. Alina grabs his hand and pulls him from the closet. She pulls the young boy close to her like a mother would when caring for her own. "Are you okay?' She asks the young kid in a nurturing like manner. The young boy doesn't say anything. He just hugs onto her. She takes her hand and rubs the back of the boy's head. "We have to go." Lamar says. They all gather themselves and prepare to exit out the front door. As they approach the door they can hear footsteps and chatter on the other side. Lamar pauses and steps back. He signals for Alina and the young one to go and hide. As they do so, Lamar sprints over toward the door and stands behind it. The door opens from outside. Lamar knows it's one of the enforcers returning to check on Vapex's status. The enforcer calls out "Vapex!" but he doesn't get a response in return. The enforcer once again yells "Vapex!" he still doesn't receive a response. Lamar remains silent while hiding behind the door. The enforcer then begins to walk through the door, then suddenly the sound of a helicopter engine being powered up cuts through the silence. The enforcer continues to walk forward. Lamar sees his opportunity for an attack just as the enforcer steps further into the hall of the compound. Lamar's eyes widen as he pushes the door shut. The enforcer attempts to turn around in reaction from the door being shut, but he's too slow to react from Lamar's brute attack. As Lamar sprints to him, he quickly disables him with a quick strike to the neck region. The enforcer's body drops to the floor immediately. Lamar then picks up the enforcer's assault rifle. He then calls out Alina and the young boy. They both come out. They quickly make their way to the door. Lamar looks through the peephole of the door. He sees there's another enforcer making his way to the entrance. Lamar with a keen stare in his eyes opens the door quickly and aims at the enforcer. He fires off two rounds that pierce through the enforcer's body. The enforcer is caught by surprised as he drops his weapon and falls flat on his face. Lamar's focus switches to the helicopter and notices Verizio is inside. He makes eye contact with him. Verizio is surprised by the fact that Lamar is still alive. Verizio then signals for the pilot of the chopper to take off. Lamar then takes the assault rifle and begins to fire at the helicopter. None of the rounds are able to pierce through the bulletproof frame of the vehicle. The chopper then levitates from the ground and accelerates. As the chopper ascends, Verizio signals to the pilot to take aim and shoot at Lamar, Alina and the young boy. "Take them out." Verizio says to the pilot. Lamar notices and shouts "Run!" They begin to sprint for cover. As they run the helicopter begins to fire off many rounds from its high-powered guns. The high-speed rounds rip through the frame of the compound; transforming the brick and wooded exterior of the compound into dust and smoke. Lamar, Alina and the young boy manage to take cover between one of the parked cars and a barricade made of stone. Lamar looks up. He tells Alina and the young one to stay put. He stands to his feet and takes off. As he's running for cover, the helicopter again begins to fire off rounds of projectiles, but Lamar manages to dodge the many rounds being fired at him as they hit and make contact with the grass and pavement. Causing debris from the dirt and concrete to pop up and fly.

Lamar makes his way behind a tree in the nearby wooded area. The tree is barely thick enough withstand the heavy-duty rounds being fired from the chopper's guns. He knows the tree won't hold up much longer. "I have to figure out a way to get her and the young one away from here." Lamar says as he peeks around the other side and gains the attention of the pilot. "I have to move quickly, long enough to allow time for them to escape." He says. He signals to Alina and the young one to make their way into one of the nearby cars to escape. He then makes his move. As he does so, the shots from the chopper began to fire off again. As Lamar sprints throughout the massive field he looks back and watches as Alina and the young boy get into one of the cars and begin to drive off. Suddenly the rounds from the helicopter's guns stop. "Something is wrong." He says to himself. He cuts his attention back to the chopper and notices it has turned around to follow Alina and the young boy. "No" He shouts out. Lamar takes off in the direction of where the helicopter is heading. Lamar with assault rifle in hand continues to run. He knows the rounds from the AK won't pierce through the armor exterior of the vehicle. "I have to figure out something." He says, as he gets close enough. He looks up and notices the chopper arming one of its missiles. The missile is engaged and ready to be fired at its target; the all black car Alina and the young boy are in. Lamar then says, "That's it." He then positions himself by taking a knee and taking aim with the assault rifle. He knows his timing has to be perfect. Just as the chopper releases its armed missile, Lamar immediately pulls the trigger and shoots at the flying missile.

The rounds come close to nailing the projectile, but they barely pass by. As the missile gets closer to the car, Lamar knows his window of opportunity is closing. He quickly focuses in and shoots. Suddenly the missile destructs while in route. The force from the explosion knocks the car over on its side. Lamar sees this and knows that they are in a terrible state. He sprints over to the car and climbs up on the topside quickly. Meanwhile the helicopter begins to circle around to re-position itself. Lamar breaks through the glass window with the butt of the assault rifle. He extends his hand down to Alina. She reaches up to make contact with his hand. She's slightly dazed by the impact of the blast. She grabs the young boy from the back of the sedan and pulls him up. Lamar pulls the young one from the wreckage and holds him close with his left arm hugged around the boy while he extends his right hand down. Alina grabs his hand and Lamar begins to pull her up. Suddenly the sound of a second missile exploding breaks through sending Lamar and the young boy flying from the top side of the car through the air and into the compound through one of the glass windows. Lamar wraps his arms around the young boy as they both tumble eventually coming to a hard stop slamming Lamar's back into the wall. He ignores the pain momentarily while he checks to see if the boy is okay. He looks down at the young one. The boy looks back with a frantic stare. Meanwhile the helicopter blades continue to chop through the air. Inside the vehicle the pilot asks Verizio "You want me to check it out?" Verizio is silent for a few seconds while he stares at the wreckage and smiles. 'There's no need." Verizio says then pauses. He then pats the pilot on his back and says, "Let's go!" The pilot then shifts the chopper around and takes off from the chaotic scene. Back inside the compound Lamar gets to his feet and looks through the window and watches as the helicopter flies away. He then limps over to the window. He climbs through the shattered glass frame and makes his way over to the wreckage of the car. He notices the car is not charred from the blast, but it's turned upside down. He gets over to the over turned vehicle. He crouches down and looks in. Inside Alina lies with her eyes closed. Lamar reaches in and grabs her by the shoulders and pulls her from the wreckage. At the moment he does not know if she is dead or alive. He sits with her head on his lap and comforts her. He rubs his fingers through her hair and hugs her close to his chest, while resting the side of his face to her forehead. Lamar with a slight bit of tears in his eyes kisses her on the forehead and softly rubs his hand under her chin. Alina eyes began to slowly open. She breathes out. Lamar in surprise looks down at her and smiles in relief. She stares back at him and smiles back. "You okay?" he asks. She remains silent for a moment and smiles "I'm fine." She says. He then helps her to her feet. "Where's the boy?" She asks. "He's over there." Lamar says as he points to the window where the young boy stands and stares.

"So where do we go from here?" Alina asks. Lamar thinks for a moment and then comes to a conclusion. "We have to separate." He says. She turns and stares at him in surprise. "It's just not safe for us to be around one another right now. I don't want to see you get harmed along the way." Lamar explains. "Make sure you get the boy to a safe place." He says. "I know a place." She responds. "When will we see one another again?" She asks. "Soon, very soon" He says. They stare into one another's eyes for a long time. Alina then leans in and they both lock lips. The kiss is passionate between the two. It's as if they're sharing their last kiss with one another. They grasp one another's hands and slowly pull away from each other. Alina then walks over to the young boy and places her hand on his head. They begin to walk off to one of the parked cars that still remain. Alina assists the young one into the back seat. As she slowly walks around to the driver side door, she begins to smile as a tear comes from her eye. She opens the door, but before she enters the car she turns, stares at Lamar and winks at him. He winks back in return. She then enters the car, starts it up, backs out the parking space and proceeds to drive off into the vanishing point of the scene. Lamar then says "No worries, we'll see each other again." He then turns to the leftover ruckus and stares at the destruction.

"THREE MONTHS LATER"

The interior setting of a lofty and comfortable home within the Tribeca section of Manhattan sets off the scene. In front of a television sits Verizio in his cozy robe, smoking one of his fancy cigars. He exhales the smoke out. He's calm for the moment. Suddenly the phone next to his comfy chair rings. He reaches over casually and picks up. "Yes" He answers. The source on the other side speaks out. "Have you heard or seen the news?" The mysterious person on the other end asks. Verizio sits up in his chair in suspicion as to what the mysterious person is speaking of. "What news are you speaking of?" Verizio blurts out. "Turn to one of the news channels and see for your self." The source says. Verizio grabs the remote next to the phone and changes the channel to CNN. The anchor's voice comes through the television in a tone of excitement. "This just in, the Chicago police department have arrested a man who is believed to be connected with more than one hundred assassinations throughout the world. He is believed to be in connection with an organization of other assassins. Police say

The Regime

Lamar Jackson turned himself into authorities this morning." The anchor explains. Verizio puts the phone down in shock of the news that he has just been informed of. He picks the phone up and puts it back to his ear. The source on the other end speaks. "I thought you took care of this." He says. Verizio remains silent. "We can't afford to have our society jeopardized over your failures!" The mysterious man says. Verizio cuts his eyes to the phone and says "Don't worry; I'll take care of it." "Hmm, I hope so, because the other Six will take care of you." The man says. "You listen to me! I run this operation, not you or the others. Me! It's my decision!" Verizio yells out. "We'll see who's in power if you fail" The source says. The phone then hangs up. Verizio is then filled with anger as he slams the phone down on the ringer.

"THE VERDICT"

The inside of the courtroom is quiet and antsy. Lamar sits on the bench with shackles and chains. "Will the defendant please rise." The judge demands. Lamar stands to his feet. "Due to the defendant pleading to all ninety eight counts of murder. I here by sentence you to consecutive life sentences without the possibility of parole at a federal prison in an disclosed location." The judge says as he slams his gable down on the mallet.

Somewhere in the snowy Rocky Mountains deep in the crust of Colorado sits a prison facility that is heavily guarded by military personal armed with heavy weaponry. Inside the facility Lamar sits in his cell with his hands together in silence. He lifts his head up as a correctional officer walks up to the cell with a tray of food in hand. "Dinner time!" The officer yells out. Lamar lifts his head up with a sinister stare in his eyes and looks on while remaining silent…

TO BE CONTINUED